The Environment

Other books in the Social Issues Firsthand series:

The Environment

Mary Hill, Book Editor

GREENHAVEN PRESS

An imprint of Thomson Gale, a part of The Thomson Corporation

Detroit • New York • San Francisco • San Diego • New Haven, Conn.
Waterville, Maine • London • Munich

Bonnie Szumski, *Publisher*
Helen Cothran, *Managing Editor*
Scott Barbour, *Series Editor*

© 2006 Thomson Gale, a part of The Thomson Corporation.

Thomson and Star Logo are trademarks and Gale and Greenhaven Press are registered trademarks used herein under license.

For more information, contact: Greenhaven Press
27500 Drake Rd.
Farmington Hills, MI 48331-3535
Or you can visit our Internet site at http://www.gale.com

LIBRARY OF CONGRESS CATALOGING-IN-PUBLICATION DATA

The environment / Mary Hill, book editor
    p. cm. -- (Social issues firsthand)
    Includes bibliographical references and index.
    0-7377-2907-4 (lib. : alk. paper)
    1. Environmentalism. 2. Environmental justice. 3. Environmentalism--
Religious aspects. 4. Environmental sciences--Social aspects. I. Hill, Mary,
1923– II. Series.
    GE195.E557 2006
    333.72--dc22
                                                            2005055138

Printed in the United States of America
10 9 8 7 6 5 4 3 2 1

Contents

A peace activist describes his belief that if people develop more loving feelings for themselves and others, they will also feel called to take better care of the planet.

Chapter Three: Environmental Ethics and Justice

Chapter Four: Environmental Activism

Foreword

Social issues are often viewed in abstract terms. Pressing challenges such as poverty, homelessness, and addiction are viewed as problems to be defined and solved. Politicians, social scientists, and other experts engage in debates about the extent of the problems, their causes, and how best to remedy them. Often overlooked in these discussions is the human dimension of the issue. Behind every policy debate over poverty, homelessness, and substance abuse, for example, are real people struggling to make ends meet, to survive life on the streets, and to overcome addiction to drugs and alcohol. Their stories are ubiquitous and compelling. They are the stories of everyday people—perhaps your own family members or friends—and yet they rarely influence the debates taking place in state capitols, the national Congress, or the courts.

The disparity between the public debate and private experience of social issues is well illustrated by looking at the topic of poverty. Each year the U.S. Census Bureau establishes a poverty threshold. A household with an income below the threshold is defined as poor, while a household with an income above the threshold is considered able to live on a basic subsistence level. For example, in 2003 a family of two was considered poor if its income was less than $12,015; a family of four was defined as poor if its income was less than $18,810. Based on this system, the bureau estimates that 35.9 million Americans (12.5 percent of the population) lived below the poverty line in 2003, including 12.9 million children below the age of eighteen.

Commentators disagree about what these statistics mean. Social activists insist that the huge number of officially poor Americans translates into human suffering. Even many families that have incomes above the threshold, they maintain, are likely to be struggling to get by. Other commentators insist that the statistics exaggerate the problem of poverty in the United States. Compared to people in developing countries, they point out, most so-called poor families have a high quality of life. As stated by journalist Fidelis Iyebote, "Cars are owned by 70 percent of 'poor' households. . . . Color televisions belong to 97 percent of the 'poor' [and] videocassette recorders belong to nearly 75 percent. . . . Sixty-four percent have microwave ovens, half own a stereo system, and over a quarter possess an automatic dishwasher."

However, this debate over the poverty threshold and what it means is likely irrelevant to a person living in poverty. Simply put, poor people do not need the government to tell them whether they are poor. They can see it in the stack of bills they cannot pay. They are aware of it when they are forced to choose between paying rent or buying food for their children. They become painfully conscious of it when they lose their homes and are forced to live in their cars or on the streets. Indeed, the written stories of poor people define the meaning of poverty more vividly than a government bureaucracy could ever hope to. Narratives composed by the poor describe losing jobs due to injury or mental illness, depict horrific tales of childhood abuse and spousal violence, recount the loss of friends and family members. They evoke the slipping away of social supports and government assistance, the descent into substance abuse and addiction, the harsh realities of life on the streets. These are the perspectives on poverty that are too often omitted from discussions over the extent of the problem and how to solve it.

Greenhaven Press's Social Issues Firsthand series provides a forum for the often-overlooked human perspectives on society's most divisive topics of debate. Each volume focuses on one social issue and presents a collection of ten to sixteen narratives by those who have had personal involvement with the topic. Extra care has been taken to include a diverse range of perspectives. For example, in the volume on adoption, readers will find the stories of birth parents who have given up their children for adoption, adoptive parents, and adoptees themselves. After exposure to these varied points of view, the reader will have a clearer understanding that adoption is an intense, emotional experience full of joyous highs and painful lows for all concerned.

The debate surrounding embryonic stem cell research illustrates the moral and ethical pressure that the public brings to bear on the scientific community. However, while nonexperts often criticize scientists for not considering the potential negative impact of their work, ironically the public's reaction against such discoveries can produce harmful results as well. For example, although the outcry against embryonic stem cell research in the United States has resulted in fewer embryos being destroyed, those with Parkinson's, such as actor Michael J. Fox, have argued that prohibiting the development of new stem cell lines ultimately will prevent a timely cure for the disease that is killing Fox and thousands of others.

Each book in the series contains several features that enhance its usefulness, including an in-depth introduction, an annotated table of contents, bibliographies for further research, a list of organizations to contact, and a thorough index. These elements—combined with the poignant voices of people touched by tragedy and triumph—make the Social Issues Firsthand series a valuable resource for research on today's topics of political discussion.

Introduction

> *"I went to the woods because I wished to live deliberately, to front only the essential facts of life, and see if I could not learn what it had to teach, and not, when I came to die, discover that I had not lived."*
>
> *—Henry David Thoreau*

Poet and essayist Henry David Thoreau wrote these words in 1845 in *Walden*. He had decided to spend twenty-six months living alone in a cabin that he built on Walden Pond in Massachusetts. Published almost a decade after his experiment, *Walden* describes his time living with only the essentials, away from the civilization he found increasingly destructive. His stated goal was to learn to live in harmony with nature. He writes, "Every morning was a cheerful invitation to make my life of equal simplicity, and I may say innocence, with Nature herself."[1]

As a conservationist who advocated the preservation of wilderness on public and private lands, Thoreau wrote many other pieces outlining his ideals for the conservation of nature. His opening words to his well-known essay "Walking" introduce his belief that humanity needs to deepen its connection with the environment:

> I wish to speak a word for nature, for absolute Freedom and Wildness, as contrasted with a freedom and Culture merely civil,—to regard man as an inhabitant, or a part and parcel of Nature, rather than a member of society. I wish to make an extreme statement, if so I may make an emphatic one, for there are enough champions of civilization; the minister, and the school-committee, and every one of you will take care of that.[2]

Later in the essay Thoreau describes what he considers the threat of developing towns and cities to the previously pristine environment of the United States. He writes, "Nowadays almost all man's improvements, so called, as the building of houses and the cutting down of the forest and of all large trees, simply deform the landscape, and make it more and more tame and cheap."[3]

Although Thoreau was not the first American to write about nature, his essays began a tradition of environmental writing that explores the relationship between human culture and nature. Today hundreds of writers pen their thoughts about nature and society's treatment of the environment. Many of these writers also often explore their sense of spiritual connection to the earth and nature.

Barry Lopez is one writer who explores these spiritual connections by writing stories and essays that focus on the natural world. He explains that since his childhood, nature and wildlife have filled him with a profound sense of the sacredness of life. He writes,

> I first felt what we could call a "state of awe," moments recognizing a metaphysical dimension in landscapes, when I was six or seven years old. I remember at the Grand Canyon, in particular, when I was eight years old, being awestruck about everything that was around me, the richness— the smells, the tackiness of ponderosa sap, the tenacity of wildflowers, those little ear tufts on the Kaibab squirrels . . . the first mountain lion I saw was in the Grand Canyon, and it was an incident that went to the floor of my heart.[4]

In many of his award-winning books and personal narratives, Lopez writes that viewing animals in the wild can reveal the spiritual dimensions of nature. In his essay "The Language of Animals," he describes living on the western slopes of the Cascade Range in Oregon. Lopez walks in the woods and along the creeks, he writes, listening to the songs of the finches and the wrens and observing the otters sunning themselves on a rock. He notes that these encounters with animals and nature give him a sense that they are connected to a source of wisdom and life that humans have abandoned but can regain.

Lopez refines this theme of exploring the spiritual awareness to be found in nature and animals in a more recent essay. He discusses how becoming connected to a landscape can provide people with an understanding that they are part of a benevolent universe that continues to evolve:

> If you're intimate with a place, a place with whose history you're familiar, and you establish an ethical conversation with it, the implication that follows is this: the place knows you're there. It feels you. You will not be forgotten, cut off, abandoned. . . . The key, I think, is to become vulnerable to a place. If you open yourself up, you can build intimacy. Out of such intimacy may come a sense of belonging, a sense of not being isolated in the universe.[5]

Another author who focuses on the spiritual experience of nature is Terry Tempest Williams. The recent recipient of the National Wildlife Federation's Conservation Award for Special Achievement, Williams began her career focusing on the desert of Utah. Much of her work examines how nature shapes spiritual beliefs. In her book *Leap* she writes, "Spiritual beliefs are not alien from Earth but rise out of its very soil. Perhaps our first gestures of humility and gratitude were extended to Earth through prayer—the recognition that we exist by the grace of something beyond ourselves. Call it God; call it Wind; call it a thousand different names."[6]

She reiterates this theme in an interview with Julie Wortman in the magazine *Witness*. Williams speaks of how the forces of nature affect her spiritual development, noting that "Wind—spirit—sculpts us, sculpts our character, our consciousness, in ways we can't even know. I am shaped differently from others because of the spiritual processes that have formed me. There is physical erosion that goes on in the desert and spiritual erosion that goes on in our search for the truth, however we define that for ourselves."[7]

Like Lopez, Williams writes about her encounters with wild animals and birds and the sense of spiritual awakening that these experiences give her. When she visited the Arctic National Wildlife Refuge in Alaska, Williams was inspired by an Arctic tern foraging by the river:

> While everyone is sleeping, the presence of this tern hovering above the river, alive, alert, engaged, becomes a vision of what is possible. . . . I will remember her. No creature on Earth has spent more time in daylight than this species. No creature on Earth has shunned darkness in the same way as the Arctic tern. No creature carries the strength and delicacy of determination on its back like this slight bird. If air is the medium of the Spirit, then the Arctic tern is its messenger.[8]

Both Barry Lopez and Terry Tempest Williams write firsthand accounts about the environment to encourage their readers to appreciate wild landscapes. They also hope to inspire people to work to protect the environment. As Williams stated in an interview, the goal of her work is "to help our culture fall in love again with language and stillness and slowness, believing that this will enable us to make better, more sustainable decisions about how to live on the planet."[9] In *Social Issues Firsthand: The Environment*, a variety of authors also present their reflections about their relationship to the environment and the best ways for society to take care of the natural world.

Notes

1. Henry David Thoreau, *Walden.* Ed. J. Lyndon Shanley. Princeton, NJ: Princeton University Press, 1971.
2. Henry David Thoreau, "Walking," The Thoreau Reader Online, August 7, 2005. http://eserver.org/thoreau/walking.html.
3. Thoreau, "Walking."
4. Quoted in Kenneth Margolis, "Paying Attention: An Interview with Barry Lopez," EnviroArts: Orion Online. http://arts.envirolink.org/interviews_and_conversations/BarryLopez.html.

5. Barry Lopez, "A Literature of Place," EnviroArts: Orion Online. http://arts.envirolink.org/literary_arts/BarryLopez_LitofPlace.html.

6. Terry Tempest Williams, *Leap*. New York: First Vintage Books, 2000.

7. Quoted in Julie A. Wortman, "Erosional Spirituality: An Interview with Terry Tempest Williams," *Witness*, April 2001. http://thewitness.org/archive/april2001/williamsinterview.html.

8. Terry Tempest Williams, "Ground Truthing: An Open Journal from the Arctic," Orion Online, May/June 2004. www.oriononline.org/pages/om/04-3om/TempestWilliams.html.

9. Quoted in Scott Slovic, "There's Something About Your Voice I Cannot Hear: Environmental Literature, Public Policy, and Ecocriticism," *Southerly*, Summer 2004.

SOCIAL ISSUES
FIRSTHAND

CHAPTER 1

Cultural Heritage and the Environment

A Native American Perspective on Nature

Elizabeth Woody

Elizabeth Woody received the American Book Award for her col-lection of poetry Hand into Stone. *She is the director of the In-digenous Leadership program for Ecotrust, a nonprofit organiza-tion promoting conservation of salmon and Native American heritage as well as restoration of coastal temperate rain forests in the northwestern United States and Canada. This excerpt is from an essay adapted from the book* Salmon Nation: People, Fish, and Our Common Home. *In the piece Woody writes about lost waterfalls in Oregon known as the Celilo Falls or Wyam. Creation of the Dalles Dam in 1957 led to the submer-sion of the falls. She remembers the tales of the falls and how important they were to the life cycle of the salmon, which her people, the Wyampum, depended upon for survival. She writes that the loss of the falls is a lesson for ecologists and environ-mentalists today and illustrates the need to protect the delicate balance of fragile ecosystems.*

Along the mid–Columbia River ninety miles east of Port-land, Oregon, stand Celilo Indian Village and Celilo Park. Beside the eastbound lanes of Interstate 84 are a peaked-roof longhouse and a large metal building. The houses in the vil-lage are older, and easy to overlook. You can sometimes see nets and boats beside the homes, though some houses are empty. By comparison, the park is frequently filled with lively and colorful wind surfers. Submerged beneath the shimmer-ing surface of the river lies Celilo Falls, or Wyam.

Wyam means "Echo of Falling Water" or "Sound of Water upon the Rocks." Located on the fourth-largest North Ameri-

Elizabeth Woody, *First Fish, First People*. Seattle: University of Washington Press, 2004. Copyright © 2004 by the University of Washington Press. Reproduced by permis-sion.

can waterway, it was one of the most significant fisheries of the Columbia River system. In recent decades the greatest irreversible change occurred in the middle Columbia as the Celilo site was inundated by The Dalles Dam on March 10, 1957. The tribal people who gathered there did not believe it possible.

Historically, the Wyampum lived at Wyam for over twelve thousand years. Estimates vary, but Wyam is among the longest continuously inhabited communities in North America. The elders tell us we have been here from time immemorial.

Today we know Celilo Falls as more than a lost landmark. It was a place as revered as one's own mother. The story of Wyam's life is the story of the salmon, and of my own ancestry. I live with the forty-two year absence and silence of Celilo Falls, much as an orphan lives hearing of the kindness and greatness of his or her mother.

The original locations of my ancestral villages on the N'chiwana (Columbia River) are Celilo Village and the Wishram village that nestled below the petroglyph, She-Who-Watches or Tsagaglallal. My grandmother, Elizabeth Thompson Pitt (Mohalla), was a Wyampum descendent and a Tygh woman. My grandfather, Lewis Pitt (Wa Soox Site), was a Wasco, Wishram, and Watlala man. But my own connections to Celilo Falls are tenuous at best. I was born two years after Celilo drowned in the backwaters of The Dalles Dam.

My grandfather fished at Celilo with his brother, George Pitt II, at a site that a relative or friend permitted, as is their privilege. They fished on scaffolds above the white water with dip nets. Since fishing locations are inherited, they probably did not have a spot of their own. They were Wascopum, not Wyampum.

When the fish ran, people were wealthy. People from all over the country would come to Celilo to watch the "Indians" catch fish. They would purchase fish freshly caught. It was one of the most famous tourist sites in North America. And many long-time Oregonians and Washingtonians today differentiate themselves from newcomers by their fond memories of Celilo Falls.

Tragedy of Loss

What happened at Wyam was more significant than entertainment. During the day, women cleaned large amounts of finely cut fish and hung the parts to dry in the heat of the arid landscape. So abundant were the fish passing Wyam on their upriver journey that the fish caught there could feed a whole family through the winter. Many families had enough salmon to trade with other tribes or individuals for specialty items.

No one would starve if they could work. Even those incapable of physical work could share other talents. It was a dignified existence. Peaceful, perhaps due in part to the sound of the water that echoed in people's minds and the negative ions produced by the falls. Research has shown this to generate a feeling of well-being in human beings. It is with a certain sense of irony that I note companies now sell machines to generate such ions in the homes of those who can "afford" this feeling of well-being.

An elder woman explained that if my generation knew the language, we would have no questions. We would hear these words directly from the teachings and songs. From time immemorial, the Creator's instruction was direct and clear. Feasts and worship held to honor the first roots and berries are major events. The head and tail of the first salmon caught at Celilo is returned to N'ch-iwana. The whole community honored that catch: *One of our relatives has returned, and we consider the lives we take to care for our communities.*

The songs in the "ceremonial response to the Creator" are repeated seven times by seven drummers, a bell ringer, and people gathered in the Longhouse. Washat song is an ancient method of worship. By wearing the finest Indian dress, the dancers show respect to the Creator.

Men on the south side, women on the north, the dancers begin to move. In a pattern of a complete circle they dance sideways, counterclockwise. This ceremony symbolizes the partnership of men and women, the essential equality and balance within the four directions and the cosmos. We each have our place and our role. As a result, the Longhouse is a special place to learn.

Meanwhile, in the kitchen, women prepare the meal. Salmon, venison, edible roots, and the various berries—huckleberries and chokecherries—are the four sacred foods. More common foods are added to these significant four on portable tables. Those who gather the roots and berries are distinguished. Their selection to gather the foods is recognition of good hearts and minds. Tribal men who have hunted and fished are likewise acknowledged. One does not gather food without proper training, so as not to disrupt natural systems.

Ignorance of the Land

What has happened to Celilo Falls illustrates a story of inadequacy and ignorance of this land. The story begins, of course, long before the submergence of the falls with the seed of ambitions to make an Eden where Eden was not needed. One needs to learn from the land how to live upon it.

The mainstem N'ch-iwana is today broken up by nineteen hydroelectric dams, many planned and built without a thought for the fish. Nuclear, agricultural, and industrial pollution, the evaporation of water from the reservoirs impounded behind dams, the clearcut mountainsides—all are detrimental to salmon. Since 1855, the N'ch-iwana's fourteen million wild salmon have dwindled to fewer than one hundred thousand.

Traditional awareness counsels in a simple, direct way to take only what we need, and let the rest grow. How can one learn? My uncle reminded me that we learned about simplicity first. He said, "The stories your grandmother told. Remember when she said her great grandmother, Kah-Nee-Ta, would tell her to go to the river and catch some fish for the day? Your grandmother would catch several fish, because she loved to look at them. She would let all but two go. Her grandmother taught her that."

A larger sorrow shadows my maternal grandmother's story of the childhood loss of the material and intangible. What if the wild salmon no longer return? I cannot say whether we have the strength necessary to bear this impending loss.

The salmon, the tree, and even Celilo Falls (Wyam) echo within if we become still and listen. Once you have heard, take only what you need and let the rest go.

Ranchers Struggle to Maintain Their Way of Life

Laura Pritchett

In this excerpt environmental writer Laura Pritchett pens a personal account of ranchers' attempts to save their land from encroaching development by harvesting rock covered with ancient lichen from their lands. The ranchers sell the rock to companies that dig it up, haul it away, and sell it to landscape and garden companies. The removal of the ancient boulders from ranchers' land could have unseen ecological impacts, she writes. Ranchers, however, need the money generated by rock sales to hold onto their culture, she concludes. Pritchett is the author of the novel Sky Bridge *(2006), and a collection of short stories,* Hell's Bottom, Colorado *(2001), which won the Milkweed National Fiction Prize and the PEN USA Award for Fiction. Her work focuses on land use issues and ranch preservation in the West and has appeared in numerous magazines, including the* Sun, Orion, High Country News, Colorado Review, divide, 5280, *and in the book* Comeback Wolves: Western Writers Welcome the Wolf Home.

Squint and shade my eyes: that's the first thing I do after scrambling out of the beat-up pickup I've been bouncing in for an hour. Squint and shade my eyes and take a deep, gut-settling breath. Light pulses from a sky so blue it vibrates, heat presses down, the air is crisp-hot and dry. It is six o'clock on a September morning, but already the Earth has forgotten what it is like to be cool in this time of drought and soaring temperatures.

Before me spreads the Weaver Ranch, the largest Angus outfit in Colorado. The family has four ranches, in fact, this one nearly six thousand acres. If I look north I can see just about all the way to Wyoming—almost a hundred miles of foothills, pastureland, desert. This is the sort of ranch that by the owner's own admission isn't going to be around for much longer. Resting just north of Fort Collins, this is the ranch that holds development at bay. From the south, ranchettes, and behind them subdivisions, are moving this way.

The owners want to hang on for a while. They love ranching, but ranching doesn't pay the bills. Standing beside the truck, I cannot see any of the Weavers' famous black cattle, just wildflowers, prickly pear cactus, sagebrush, various grasses turned yellow, a few small shrubs, and a lot of rock. This foothill is blanketed in sandstone, and all the rock is covered in moss—or, to be accurate, lichen. "Moss rocks" are the Weavers' new commodity. And the rocks are why we're here.

My friend Tim goes for the JCB, a forklift with extendable arms. It roars into action, and my brother David starts unloading pallets and chicken wire from the back of the truck. I busy myself doing what I've been told to do, picking up smaller rocks from the hillside and heaving them on the pile to fill in between the larger stones. I look for the biggest rocks I can lift, ones with a lot of lichen. I'm not a very efficient worker because I keep stopping to look off toward the horizon, or peer at a bug scuttling off as I take away its cover.

Making Rocks Work

Tim drives toward us with a rock weighing a few hundred pounds and maneuvers the forklift's arms to set it on the pallet while David directs him with hand gestures. The engine whines, a rock thumps, both of them yell, and the landscape changes a little, then a little more, as rocks are moved from the hillside and stacked on the pallet.

During breaks, when Tim turns off the forklift, they discuss whether a particular patch of sage-green lichen is a species they've seen before or some other species, how and why they do rock work, why two college graduates would *want* to do this work, and whether they have any qualms about the ecological damage they are doing. This last part is for my benefit. They know I've tagged along today to try to understand how tearing up the landscape might be a good thing.

"We're creating value," Tim argues, though I haven't said anything. "We take something worth absolutely nothing, and with our sweat, we make it worth something. Isn't that sort of amazing?"

"We make the rocks work, so to speak."

"When we take the really big rocks, they leave holes."

"But within a few months they're filled with native grasses."

"We always leave tipi rings alone. Always."

"It just depends on how it's done, like with everything."

"Look, there's tons of this rock. We take it out, we make more grazing space, the rancher gets extra money, this keeps the rancher in business, so development gets slowed down."

"Yup."

"Good for nature in the long run," David says with a wink. He offers this just to bug me, his "eco-extreme sister," as he's fond of calling me, and to get in the last jab.

Selling Rock to Hold onto Land

As the day wears on, we talk less. Our energies are spent wiping the sweat off our foreheads, keeping going in the fierce heat. Tim and David work hard, but I don't hear any grumbling. Neither of them lasted long at their white-collar jobs (Tim as a pilot, David as a microbiologist). My guess is that it was because they'd rather be out here, where the sunlight streaks down from a turquoise sky, the view stretches for miles, and the rest of humanity is far away.

Up the hill from me is a rock nearly as tall as I am, covered in three kinds of lichen, and weighing, by Tim's estimate, about seven tons. According to the equation he has just explained, this rock will sell for about $700 (though some go for several thousand), the Weavers will make about $70, and the laborer who moves it—David or Tim or someone like them—will get about $15 per hour, the company he works for getting the rest. Ten dollars a ton doesn't sound like much to me. I wonder aloud how mining moss rock is going to keep ranchers in the black. Tim reminds me that rock is heavy and there's a lot of it. He guesses that this ranch took in maybe $60,000 from moss rocks last year, or "at least enough to cover their taxes."

I look out across the buckles and rises of earth in front of me. I know that ranchers like the Weavers hang on to their land out of love, not good economic sense, because they could make millions developing it. Cow-calf operators in Colorado have operated on slim margins for years. Despite my highfalutin environmental ethics, I can see why a family that has spent decades struggling to make ends meet might find it hard to look millions of dollars in the face and turn away.

And so they sell; agricultural land in western states declines at an average of one million acres a year. I know a few ranchers who have sold out—*Can't ranch with development all around me, getting old, can't stop change, kids don't want the place,* they tell me. And I know several who haven't, and instead put their land into conservation easements. For those who don't sell, loss is generally offset by off-ranch income from other jobs or investments, or by diversifying their operations with services or products such as outfitting, wildlife viewing, raising nontraditional animals like elk. Or selling moss rock.

A "Rock" Bonanza

The rocks from the Weaver Ranch will be taken to the Rock Yard, a large, dusty lot in Fort Collins owned by the guy who employs Tim and David. When we stopped there to get pallets and tools this morning as the sky was just turning light, I saw how neatly nature gets organized—granite rocks on one half of the lot, sandstone on the other, each group categorized by size. The biggest rocks weigh several tons and are retrieved from mountainsides with logging machines. Medium-sized rocks—about the size of a pillow—get piled on pallets and covered with chicken wire. The smallest ones are stashed in a cage built from concrete-reinforcing wire.

Tim and David are in the business of collecting the medium and small sizes, which mostly get sold to landscapers. The demand is at an all-time high, according to Tim, fueled primarily by urban homeowners. Besides the local market, which has surprised everyone, lots of rock gets shipped to other states, particularly Nebraska.

"Where there's no moss rock?" I ask.

"Where there's no rock," Tim answers with a chuckle. He notes that customers there pay up to three times what they do here for a piece of Colorado.

Everyone, apparently, is buying moss rock. "These rocks sell themselves," Tim says. He tells me that the government's been buying lots of the really big rocks to put outside buildings—"You know, to keep cars with bombs from smashing into government offices." A customer up I-70 has just placed an order for four hundred tons; he'll sell it to a developer for landscaping. Another order's just come in from "some rich guy who wants shadows."

"Shadows?"

"Yeah. To put near his house, pretend he's in a canyon, I don't know. He asked for rocks that throw good shadows." Tim shrugs. The aesthetic sense of some customers is beyond his comprehension, but we both understand this much: the rocks are beautiful.

"All those orders will wipe this out," Tim says, waving his hand over the boulder-strewn foothill. "But that's okay. There's more where it came from."

Tim gets back on the JCB and brings more and more rocks from the slope to the pallet. When the pile begins to get high, four feet or so, David guides the rocks here and there, turns them around. Tim gets out of the forklift to help him and they have a long consultation on placement, argue a little, and turn the rocks around some more. They are positioning them so the moss shows, since the buyer will only see the exposed sides, but they are also being careful to balance the rocks just so. It seems that some moss rock fell off a truck on I-25 recently, killing a person in the car behind it.

"But it wasn't our moss rock," says David.

"God, I'd hate to see that," says Tim. And they go back to their balancing act.

Once a pallet is full (as high as the rock pile can go while remaining stable), it will weigh about a ton and a half. As Tim starts on the next one, David surrounds the rocks on the first with chicken wire. He nails the wire to the pallet with roofing nails, then uses a hay hook to twist it tight. The job is done: a bundle of moss rock caged up, a chunk of western rangeland ready to be shipped and placed in someone's garden or patio.

I try to picture these jailed rocks in their new homes. That rock would make an attractive barrier, this one might cast some nice shade, and this beautiful, bumpy rock carved by wind and rain—yes, this one would look wonderful in *my* garden.

Rock Works Ecological Impact

The debate about the ecological impact of "rock work" is complicated, like so many land-use issues in the West. On the one hand moss-rock sales, by making ranches viable, preserve critical wildlife habitat and open space. The lichens themselves are supposedly not hurt in the move as long as they continue to receive about the same amount of sunlight, and more lichens will grow on the new rocks that are exposed, and—well, these rocks seem to be just about everywhere. On the other hand, removing the rocks disrupts a fragile ecosystem, destroying habitat for rodents and reptiles. Also, the heavy equipment used to extract the rock widens and compacts roads, and the disturbance allows weeds to flourish after native plants have been uprooted. Environmental groups such as the Sierra Club have not yet taken a formal position on the moss-rock issue.

Near the end of the day, I wander farther up the hill, my mind churning with questions. Plus, I'd like to pick up an arrowhead. They're often found out here, and my chances are pretty good since we're on a slope facing south and east—out of the wind and a likely place for a long-ago camp. All I find, though, are grass, cactus, an enormous black beetle. I stop in front of a sandstone boulder covered with pale-green and orange lichens. Although they look dead to me, dried up and baked into the rock, I know they are still growing. These lichens may be several hundred years old—roughly the same age as any arrowhead I might discover here. It occurs to me that their age is part of what makes both of them valuable, and might be a reason not to remove either one from its home on the mountain.

Tim's cellphone rings in his truck. He takes the call and walks over to where David and I are taking a break. "Some clown down at the Rock Yard needs my help loading up a semi-truck full of rock."

He shrugs, perhaps sorry that our day out here is over, that he has to return us to town, or perhaps in acknowledgment of forces like cellphones and work schedules and the need to hold a job. David and I put the tools back in the truck, Tim parks the forklift, we all gulp water from old milk jugs.

I wipe the sweat from my neck, lean against the truck, blink my stinging eyes. The sun seeps red through my eyelids and the shapes of the land linger in dark silhouettes. As we climb into the truck, I look back at the cages of moss rock that dot the landscape. The result of our work. The rocks ready now to do *their* work, which seems to be to protect their homeland by going somewhere else.

Global Warming Threatens the Inuit Community

Sheila Watt-Cloutier

Sheila Watt-Cloutier is the chair of the Inuit Circumpolar Con-
ference (ICC), an international nongovernment organization
representing approximately 150,000 Inuit in Alaska, Canada,
Greenland, and Russia. The goals of ICC include promoting
Inuit rights and interests on an international level as well as de-
veloping and encouraging long-term policies that safeguard the
Arctic environment. For her environmental work with ICC and
on behalf of her people, Watt-Cloutier received the prestigious
Sophie Prize, an international award of $100,000 from the
Sophie Foundation, established in 1992 by Norwegian author
Jostein Gaarder and his wife Siri Dannevig. In this excerpt from
her acceptance speech for the prize, Watt-Cloutier tells the story
of the Inuit people and their environmental heritage. She argues
that toxins carried to the Arctic on air currents contaminate the
animals the Inuit hunt for food and endanger her people's way
of life. Additionally, she states that global warming causes the
Arctic ice and snow to melt, threatening the hunting culture of
the Inuit. Watt-Cloutier concludes that global warming affects
not only the Inuit but also families and communities worldwide.

L et me begin by honouring where I come from: the Inuit world. I was born into an ancient culture and have humble beginnings. So, I am moved personally and as a member of an ancient people. This prize is important to Inuit everywhere.

I am able to do global work because my culture, my hunting culture, gives me the foundation and focus I need. It is my humble beginnings connected to my hunting culture that gives me the foundation upon which I do this global work

Sheila Watt-Cloutier, "Connectivity: The Arctic—the Planet," www.inuitcircumpolar
.com, June 15, 2005. Copyright © 2005 by Sheila Watt-Cloutier. Reproduced by permission.

with a sense of focus, commitment, and tenacity. It is through this culture that draws connections to everything that I too have come to see and understand connectivity from the community level through to the globe at large.

Inuit Hunting Culture in Jeopardy

Inuit have a deep understanding of the cycles, rhythms, seasons, and natural changes in life. Living on the land requires a high level of independence, self-confidence, good judgment, initiative, and skill. In my hunting culture, challenges are very real and immediate, and this remains so today. But the skills and attitudes needed to survive on the land are transferable and highly relevant in the rapidly changing world in which we all now live.

Let me try to give you a window on my world. I am part of a generation that has experienced tumultuous change in a very short period of time. We have come from a traditional world to a high tech way of life. In 51 years I have come from traveling by dog team and canoe to flying jumbo jets all over the world. In fact this gives a new meaning to the term "coming from the ice age to space age in one generation".

This change has been at great cost to Inuit society. Our communities witness much challenges in terms of our families and communities. Our families and communities have been shaken by the change from a strong, independent way of life—living and learning from the land with our own education, judicial, social and economic systems now to a way of life highly dependent on substances, institutions and processes.

But now we are thinking. We are stopping to look at what's happening in our communities. We are starting to look at these things but more importantly we are starting to feel. We have begun to recognize what has happened in our Inuit world. We are beginning to realize the need to regain control that has been lost in recent decades—over our health and the health of our communities. We have begun to appreciate even more the importance of the wisdom of the land in regaining the health of our families and communities.

The land not only teaches technical skills of aiming the gun or harpoon or skinning a seal, it teaches what is required to survive, giving confidence to our people and it builds the character, skills of judgment, courage, patience, boldness under pressure and withstanding stress. A sense of peace. It is wisdom, ultimately that we are trying to teach our children so that they can choose life over self-destruction.

As we regain and reclaim a more sustainable way of life we realize the Arctic is being harmed by global processes. Inuit are being poisoned from afar by toxin—PCBs, DDT and other chemicals—carried to the Arctic on air currents. These chemicals contaminate the food web we depend upon (seals, whales, walruses) and end up in our bodies and the nursing milk of our mothers in high levels. So what a world we have created when Inuit women have to think twice about nursing their babies. Climate change is happening very fast in the Arctic. Our hunting culture is literally melting away as ice and snow disappears. What sad irony is this?

Inuit Survival Connected to Planet's Survival

However, powerless victims we are not. The Inuit culture not only survived but also thrived harmoniously with nature in what people call the harshest environment in the world. We invented homes of snow, warm enough for our babies to sleep in naked. We invented the *qajaag,* the most ingeniously engineered boat. Inuit won't disappear or be wiped out by globalization. Rather, we hope our destiny is to light a beacon for the world.

I think by now you see these issues are not just about the environment or wildlife; these issues are about children, families, and communities. This is about people—the cultural survival of an entire people—which, of course, are connected to the survival of the planet as a whole. What happens in the

The Inuit are facing land loss from rising sea levels caused by global warming, which is melting glaciers in their region. © Dave Bartruff/CORBIS

Arctic is important to all of us. The Arctic is indeed the health barometer—the early warning—for the rest of the world.

Science and Inuit traditional knowledge agree: climate change is endangering the Arctic and the whole planet. But some won't take effective change and action. Last November [2004] all eight Arctic countries, including the United States, endorsed the Arctic Climate Impact Assessment [ACIA]— prepared over four years by more than 300 scientists from 15 countries and many Indigenous peoples, and in fact, the chair of ACIA Bob Corell is here with us today. This assessment states that our ancient connection to our hunting culture may well disappear and within my own grandson's lifetime.

So, we want to urge all the leaders of the G8 [group of eight leading world nations], and particularly President [George W.] Bush to commit to significant reductions of greenhouse gas emissions. We must go beyond Kyoto.[1] As the

1. The Kyoto Protocol, an international and legally binding agreement to reduce greenhouse emissions worldwide, went into force in February 2005. The United States has refused to ratify the agreement.

Minister indicated, Kyoto is but our first step. The place to start is Montreal in November and December at the 11th Conference of Parties to the climate change convention. It will be very important that the world get together to make effective change there and start the process.

I must also say that the European Union plan to allow for a 2 degrees Centigrade of warming will still see the destruction of Arctic ecosystems. The melting of the Greenland ice sheet will flood low-lying countries such as Bangladesh and many small island states. We cannot let fear prevent us from taking action.

Climate Change Is a Human Story

It is because climate change is a human story that we have connected climate change and human rights. We hope that the language of human rights will bridge perspectives and illustrate the seriousness of global warming. We need to capture the attention and conscience of the world, for climate change is a threat to our entire way of life, and to yours.

Inuit remain intimately connected with each other and with the land. And, is it not to reestablish that connection that we are all grappling with climate change? Is it not because people have lost the connection between themselves and their neighbors, between their actions and the environment, that we are struggling to come to grips with climate change?

There are only 155,000 Inuit in the whole world, and as I said we face many challenges, but I am blessed to have my feet firmly planted in my culture. Working from within my culture, and as Chair of the Inuit Circumpolar Conference [ICC], I am privileged to have a "birds eye view" of the challenges and opportunities out there on the horizon. . . .

When we see that as the Arctic melts the Small Island Developing States sink, we see clearly how the planet is one. It cannot get clearer than that in terms of understanding connectivity. We must also see the connections as well as the lack of balance between unsustainable economic policies adopted by some countries, and how these policies are leading to the destruction of the entire way of life of a people, the people of the Arctic.

I applaud the vision and commitment of the Government of Norway to support a five-year programme suggested by the United Nations Environment Programme office in Arendal and ICC to link Arctic interests and the Small Island Developing States. These areas are both vulnerable to climate change, and we can learn so much from one another.

As I said last fall [2004] to a committee of the US Senate:

> Global warming connects us all. Use what is happening in the Arctic as a vehicle to connect us all, so that we may understand that the planet and its people are one. The Inuit hunters who fall through the depleting and unpredictable sea ice are connected to the cars we drive, the industries we rely upon, and the disposable world we have become.

Keeping Up the Good Fight

This prize encourages me to keep up the good fight, so to speak, not only for our people but also for the planet. This is a time and an opportunity for all of us to recognize our shared humanity and to deepen our shared concern and commitment to the well-being of the planet. Rest assured that this prize encourages me to continue my work connecting climate change and human rights.

As our hunting culture is based on the cold, being frozen with lots of snow and ice, we thrive on it. We are in essence fighting for our right to be cold. So together let us choose to err on the side of caution rather than wait until it is too late. In further understanding connectivity, our move to link climate change and human rights is not personal in terms of targeting a specific country. It is a political strategy for the right reasons at the right time in this time in history. . . .

Where it does get personal ladies and gentlemen is at the people level, at the receiving end of pollution and the negative impacts of greenhouse gas emissions. It is personal when Inuit mothers have to worry and make difficult choices about feeding their babies and whether or not they should. It is personal when the fathers and grandfathers are now worried how they will pass down traditional knowledge and skills to our young men, young men who in our society often carry the heaviest burdens of a transitioning culture and all too often take the most drastic exits from life. "Human Rights" indeed.

As the mother and grandmother in me drives all that I do and leads the elected leader in me and I do this work for the future of my precious grandson, I want you to know I am humbly proud to accept the Sophie Prize for all of us in our Inuit home lands. I think of my young grandson. I think of his father hunting. I think of all of those young people at home who are grappling with issues and who all too often we lose so young.

I also want to take this opportunity at this time to honour and remember my family members that I have lost in the last 5 years while doing this global work. In memory of my only beloved sister, in memory of my aunt, in memory of my mother and my young cousin, I accept from my heart and soul this prize. The influence, love and support I received from these ... important women remain with me always and since their departing in the last few years I feel they have never left my side.

In that light I wish to end with a quote by an American poet named Louise Bogan whose words speak to me in the work I do.

In a time lacking in truth and certainty and filled with anguish and despair, no woman should be shamefaced in attempting to give back to the world through her work, a portion of its lost heart.

CHAPTER 2

Nature and Spirituality

Nature Provides a Sanctuary for Reflection

Cindy Crosby

In this selection nature essayist Cindy Crosby writes about her spiritual experience as she walks in the Schulenberg Prairie at the Morton Arboretum in Illinois. She compares the plight of the prairie compass plants to her own struggles with self-doubt and shortcomings. She writes that just as insects attack the compass plants, bad decisions riddle her life. In the end, though, the power of the landscape and the beauty of the bursting yellow buds of the compass plants draw her closer to God and help her find personal forgiveness. Crosby is a full-time freelance writer and the author of Waiting for Morning: Hearing God's Voice in the Darkness.

> Grass is the forgiveness of nature—her constant benediction.
>
> *—John James Ingalls, "In Praise of Blue Grass"*

> Repentance is not a popular word these days, but I believe that any of us recognize it when it strikes us in the gut. Repentance is coming to our senses, seeing, suddenly, what we've done that we might not have done, or recognizing . . . that the problem is not in what we do but in what we become.
>
> *—Kathleen Norris,* The Cloister Walk

I've regretted many things in my life, but never watching a sunset. Tonight I make time for the early evening pageantry. At home the family is fed, the dishes are washed, and the kids are busy checking e-mail and talking on the phone. Community and family are things I cherish, but after a day full of both, I'm looking forward to slipping away to the prairie for a little solitude.

As I walk through the tallgrass this evening, the sky splits open like a milkweed pod, slipping its silks into the dying light to be combed by the wind into long, cirrus strands. Tonight it backlights the acres and acres of blooming compass plants, leaves all aligned in the same direction.

Pick up any book about the prairie, and sooner or later you'll read about the compass plant, *Silphium laciniatum*. It's a prairie icon. The basal leaves are coarsely cut—deeply divided, flat, and perhaps second only to prairie dock in size. They resemble large, elongated oak leaves. The compass plant's thick, bristly stem skyrockets up to a dozen feet tall in July, overtopping the grasses and forbs, reaching for sunshine. It's topped with alternating flowerheads similar to small yellow sunflowers.

The hairy stems bleed sap, which Native Americans used as gum. I like to gather the sparkling rosin beads from the wounded stems and chew the resulting piny-tasting wad. After a little mastication, it resembles Wrigley's spearmint. If the rosin beads are newly leaked, they melt on my fingers, making them tacky as super glue. I stick to everything I come in contact with until I'm back home and able to scrub the sap off of my hands.

Dying Compass Plants

I tried to grow compass plants in my garden at home without much success—the rabbits thought I was growing a salad bar for their enjoyment—and so I consoled myself for a long time with the proliferation of compass plants out on the Schulenberg Prairie. If I couldn't have them in my backyard, then at least here.

This July, as in all Julys, the compass plants reach shoulder height and begin to bloom. But as soon as the flower-fest begins, the budding flowers start dying *en masse*.

Horrified, I examine a compass plant. Its flower stems are partially severed; the wounds leak resinous sap. The flower buds sag and are already turning to brown. All around me the same scenario is enacted. Compass plants are dying, and I don't know why.

It takes a village to answer all my questions. As was his habit, prairie manager Craig Johnson took our volunteer group on a walk at sunset one evening, after we were pleasantly exhausted from weeding the sweet white clover and ragweed. Pausing by a compass plant, half its flowers drooping, severed, and dying, he explained that the *Silphiums*, particularly the compass plant, host parasites. Among these are mordellid larvae, which tunnel through the flowering stems. As adult weevils, they clip off the compass plant blooms and lay eggs in the flowers. The dying flower head becomes their weevil nursery.

The Plants' Determination to Overcome Setbacks

All is not lost, however. Even as the weevils wreak havoc, the plant is quietly putting out another set of unspoiled buds. These wait, tight and curled, until the weevil has done its work below. Then they burst into bloom.

Compass plants have a fierce determination to overcome numerous setbacks. It makes me think of the poet May Sarton, who in her battles with depression found comfort in these lines: "I think the secret of much of the unrest and dissatisfaction with one's self and longing for a more vivid, expressive existence is the thing planted deep in everyone— turning toward the sun, the love of a virtue and splendor that must be adored. . . . One is always trying to tune one's self to an unheard perfection."

The compass plants work with what they've got, striving for perfection despite their flaws. Overcoming apparent disaster, they burst forth in as many as a hundred blooms. Their bright yellow rays illuminate the prairie like thousands of small triumphant suns, more glorious for the attacks they have weathered. When the seeds finally ripen in early October, I spend autumn afternoons watching goldfinches perched on compass plant stalks, enjoying their snacks.

A Limestone Altar

Tonight I stop and rest on the limestone ledge overlooking Willoway Brook. The air is fresh and clean smelling; the sheets of the day are hung out to dry on the line of night until morning, when they'll be shaken out to cover the landscape again. The sun's gold coin drops into the slot of the horizon as the blue sky dissolves to apricot and lavender.

These peaceful evenings on the prairie are a time of quiet self-examination. Looking at the little destructive things in my own life. Taking my faults out one by one, I relentlessly sort through them. Jealousy. Wanting what a friend has. Impatience. Anger. Failure to forgive a family member who wronged me. Serious selfishness issues. Other sins that I name silently but don't dare write in my journal. The limestone ledge becomes my confessional as I wait for God to bring each troublesome fault to light. I wrestle with the darkness in the landscape of my soul.

My shortcomings separate me from the one I want to know. Little sins that don't seem like much at the time build up until they form a logjam that freezes my communication with my creator. Recognizing my deficiencies is more difficult than it sounds—I'm an expert in cover-up, proficient in the art of delusion, rationalization.

Until things start to wither. Go wrong. Collapse. Often I'm at the point of positive change, only to abruptly lapse back into my old habits, like the compass plant flowers withering as they are trying to bloom. I feel disillusioned and disappointed and horrified by turns. It's then that a regular time of self-examination and confession induces honesty; it calls up my true shortcomings from the darkness to the light. I look at the marks on my soul, and it's the same sins I keep seeing, over and over. Ingrained habits shoved down to unfathomable levels, grooved into my psyche. Rearing their ugly heads in the light of day.

Bringing Walls Down

The seven deadly sins according to Christian tradition are pride, anger, envy, gluttony, lust, sloth, and covetousness. I have more than a nodding acquaintance with them all; and some seem to have taken up permanent residency. I acknowledge the places where I've wronged another, said a sharp word, envied a friend—all little sins, I tell myself, barely visible ones. The more time that passes while I tolerate a particular shortcoming, the more it is subtly interlaced into my life, tangling me into a net of my own construction. Just as with poison, "a regimen of small doses is usually what kills us," writes Garret Keizer in *The Enigma of Anger*. A regimen of small doses of sin has kept me from praying in the way that I long to. Their cumulative power is formidable. Burrowing into my soul, they abruptly cut off my chance to be the person I desire. To be the person I want to become, I have to deal with these sins, do some damage control.

Bringing them out into the light and grieving over my faults compels me to throw myself straight into the arms of the one who loves me most; the only one who can make me clean again. It's the first step in the elimination process: a recognition of my imperfections and a longing for grace.

"Be prepared. You're up against far more than you can handle on your own," the apostle Paul wrote. "Take all the help you can get, every weapon God has issued, so that when it's all over but the shouting, you'll still be on your feet. . . . Prayer is essential in this ongoing warfare. Pray hard and long. . . . Keep your eyes open."

Even when my eyes are open, I am tempted to wall off the pain caused by my imperfections. It's a protective mechanism. I have to unlearn this. Pull the barriers down, and let myself experience the emotions my wrongs have elicited. When at last I feel the grief of my failures, I'm ready to ask for forgiveness.

My eyes are open. The walls are coming down.

The Power of Landscape

The power of landscape excavates these emotions. Tears come easily, the thin veneer of being "on" for whoever is around is peeled away. The prairie is a safe place for me to cry. I am willing to exhale, to not "buck up and keep strong." To admit the anguish of what I've done.

What would a sinless life look like? I can only imagine. Strive as I may, I won't achieve it. My interior landscape is scarred. I identify with Sisyphus, rolling the boulder up the mountain only to watch it break from my grasp and go rolling down again. Not even three steps forward, two steps back. More like devastating falls and crashing disappointments in myself.

Occasionally I rush through confession. But to be *truly* sorry, to grieve faults, I must stop myself, find a place of quiet, and take time—time to imagine what the effect of the thing I've said, or done, or thought, has been on myself or another. Time to grasp what making even a small bad choice means. Suffering genuine sorrow. Changing my attitude. Not confessing as a selfish desire to wipe the slate clean to make myself feel better.

A Time for Confession

The most compelling aspect of the compass plant is the position of its leaves, which loosely point north and south. To see the prairie at sunset with the coarse compass plant leaves backlit by the dying light, all pointing the same direction, is to join yourself with the Native Americans who likely paused at the same portent of something greater than themselves.

I try to keep pointed in the right direction. Keep my focus on where I'm headed. Taking my cues from the compass plant, and from my time spent in self-examination.

Reformed alcoholic and former Catholic priest Brennan Manning writes:

> Confession becomes more than a "Minit-Wash," more than a sigh of relief for summoning the courage and the humility necessary for honest self-disclosure, more than mere satisfaction. . . . It becomes a joyful return to the Father's house, a reconciliation with the Christian community in a spirit of atonement and gratitude, a building of the love-relationship with God and our fellow human beings which sin had attacked, a reopening of the human heart, and a renewed possibility for the full, definitive flowering of the Christian personality in the wisdom of tenderness.

Confession followed by grieving my faults offers me this potential for a "full, definitive flowering." As [writer] Kathleen Norris, in *The Cloister Walk*, reminds me, "Repentance is valuable because it opens in us the idea of change." I've resisted change in my life, but I'm acknowledging my need for it now.

When I miss my time of confession through prayer, I'm scattered like the clouds, blown by the wind. Cast adrift. My faults, my sins, are what separate me from a God who is holy. Prayer is, as Eugene Peterson writes, "the action that integrates the inside and the outside of life." It keeps me from straying too far off course. At day's end, I pray the Daily Office's Compline, which brings me a sense of completion. It starts with confession:

> Almighty God, my heavenly Father: I have sinned against you, through my own fault, in thought, and word, and deed, and in what I have left undone. For the sake of your Son our Lord Jesus Christ, forgive me all my offenses; and grant that I may serve you in newness of life, to the glory of your Name. Amen.

Finding Renewed Faith in Nature

Confessing, spilling tears. Finding renewed faith in God's aggressive grace in the light of my shortcomings. "There is a distinct comfort in being known, is there not?" asks Keizer. It's this recognition that I am known by God—deeply known, down to all of my grubby little imperfections; that I'm welcomed and accepted by him anyway, that satisfies deep longings and comforts me in a way nothing else can do. Because of grace. "Grace ... invites us into life—a life that goes on and on and on, world without end," as Paul says in the biblical book of Romans.

Grace. Forgiveness. The bitter disappointments of my shortcomings are mitigated by both.

I immerse myself in the world's fleeting moments of beauty, glimpses of the eternal. My inner well is full, replenished each night by sunsets that break my heart, by the stamp of a deer's hoof in the twilight, by fierce owls with soft wings and claws of destruction, by cold that turns my breath into vapor that forms a cloud, then swirls away into the dark.

Desolation followed by consolation. Confession followed by inner cleansing. I entreat God in my prayers with the words from the psalmist, "Remember not our past sins; let your compassion be swift to meet us."

The day is being swallowed by the night; the cooler evening air magnifies a mouse's rustle in the tallgrass along the path into a gunshot. My steps crackle loudly on the gravel road in the dusk. As I walk back to Parking Lot 25, twilight is beginning to lacquer the landscape in grays and blacks.

I reach for my keys and lean against the car, praying Compline's ending words: "Lord, you now have set your servant free to go in peace as you have promised."

Around me, the darkness is complete. But I'm forgiven.

Discovering God in Nature

Lisa Couturier

Ecologist and essayist Lisa Couturier describes a spiritual odyssey of discovery in this essay excerpted from "Off Being God," a piece that appears in her book The Hopes of Snakes. *The focus of her essay is a controversy involving a Cleveland Zoo gorilla named Timmy. Zoo officials wanted to move Timmy to the New York City Zoo so that he could impregnate other gorillas. Cleveland citizens, however, protested because they felt Timmy already loved a Cleveland Zoo gorilla named Kate. Kate, however, was sterile. As the two sides in the case went to court, Couturier visited a charismatic Episcopalian church with two friends. She writes about the revelation she has during the service that a new kind of Christianity must be developed that does not give humans a privileged relationship with God. She questions whether humans have a right to separate two gorillas who have a special bond just because the zoo wants to breed more gorillas. An environmental journalist and former magazine editor, Couturier's essays have appeared in the* American Nature Writing series, *in* National Geographic's Heart of a Nation: Writers and Photographers Inspired by the American Landscape, *in the PBS series* Writers Writing, *and in other anthologies and magazines.*

> When I was a child, I spoke as a child, I understood as a child, I thought as a child: but when I became a man, I put away childish things.
>
> *I Corinthians 13*

Three children who cannot sit still are about to take turns holding Esther the barn owl. It is Birds of Prey Day at a school north of Manhattan; and Esther, all of a pound heavy, will perch on the thin arms of these children in front of an audience of hundreds gathered under a big white outdoor tent. Esther will hold on with her four powerful toes, two of which can turn forward and two backward. It doesn't appear to matter to the children that soon their skin will be lightly pricked with the weapons of an owl's body—the long, curved, knife-sharp talons at the ends of Esther's toes, talons she uses to snatch rodents, bats, and birds out of life, talons that plunge into the torso of a mouse and pin it to the forest floor, enabling Esther to make the fatal bite at the base of the mouse's skull with the other knife of her body, her sharp, hooked beak. The children are focused simply on holding Esther, whispering to Esther. And Esther, sleepy Esther—the white feathers of her heart-shaped face rousing beside the round and dimpled cheeks of these kids—will listen intently with her asymmetrical skull, one ear-opening nearer the top of her head than the other; but she will say nothing.

Usually, on a bright sunny morning such as this, when Esther was wild, she would be sleeping just about now—in an old building, an attic, a cemetery, a church steeple, a barn—and so there is no reason to change her ways and divulge the intricacies of meaning in what she says most often, which is not a hoot but a loud and scary-sounding *shreeee* screamed in flight. It is perhaps because of this dead-of-night habit of hers, this screaming in flight, along with her pale face and silent flying, that some call her species the ghost owl.

But facts are not concerns of the children. They, instead, are awash with the contentment that floods the body when one is considered by the dark eyes of a wild animal, an animal that seems in some way to be peering at and thinking of you. And if they are the eyes of a powerhouse animal, like a raptor, like Esther, and if you know—as the parent of a child who is about to hold an owl might—that with Esther's not inconsiderable strength she could rip the muscles out of your hands, it could be that the contentment felt in the presence of a barn owl is that brought on by what seems like the owl's compassion for your weaknesses: owl as the all-merciful.

Children in the audience, children who are not students of the school, yell out: "Can I hold Esther!?" "How many children does Esther have?" "How old is Esther?" "Please, please, I want to hold Esther!" In what they understand as their own bird sign language, the children prop out their black and white arms, stiff as branches, ready and willing for Esther to fly their way. . . .

The Flight of Falcons

After Esther's show under the big white tent, a naturalist gives a short lecture about the lives of raptors and about why some species are declining. Pesticides and toxins in water and on croplands enter the foods raptors eat: rodents, fish, small birds, and amphibians; eventually the toxins build up in the raptor, killing, if not the bird itself, the bird's ability to reproduce. Then, we have habitat loss, occurring at dizzying speeds. Next, the incidentals: power lines that electrocute birds, glass buildings into which birds crash, and, not to be forgotten, says the naturalist, the general inhumanity of humans. "We shoot. We trap. We do," he says, "the expected, deplorable things." . . .

Where the falconry tent ends, just by the bulging roots of an old oak tree, I see a large crowd gathering around the raptor I think of as ceaseless in my life: red-tailed hawk; and suddenly it is not as [German poet Rainer Maria] Rilke wrote, not "everything is far and long gone by." Since living in New York City, I have missed red-tailed hawks from the fields of my long ago, when we raced—I running along the country roads, they gliding the airstrips above. I remember the crayfishy smell of the creek under the one-lane bridge, near where foxes ran: this was where I found, anchored by its shaft in the sandy mud of the creek bank, a red-tailed feather leaning in the breeze. . . .

No matter what, a red-tailed hawk is the classic hawk, the quintessential of all magnificent soaring hawks. Undemanding—this could be said of a red-tailed, or extremely adaptable. The most recent generations of red-tailed hawks have grown up with me, or, more accurately, have grown again in numbers as I have grown. When I was born, a red-tailed hawk was rare, persecuted by environmental toxins that over the decades were outlawed. Now, some forty years later, red-tailed hawks are ubiquitous, the common roadside hawk perched along interstate medians, or, glance up, one is above you, kiting— which means hanging motionless on four-foot wingspans— over cornfields, housing developments, forest edges, and elementary schools while they hunt. . . . Actually, it would not be terribly inaccurate to say red-tailed hawks are, if not omniscient, then, omnipresent.

The crowd around the hawk does not let up. Somewhere through all the questions, I hear the falconer say the hawk's name is Majestic. I decide to wait for the crowd to dissipate, realizing I finally will meet the species of bird that, in a certain sense, gave me back my voice last summer.

Timmy's Story

It was August in Cleveland, and I had flown in from New York to cover a story about Timmy, a gorilla who many Clevelanders believed was in love with another gorilla named Kate. The issue brewing about the gorillas was the imminent decision by zoo officials to move Timmy to a zoo in New York City, where, officials believed, Timmy ultimately would have a better and more prosperous conjugal life, a sort of multiple-choice life, with several female gorillas living in the Bronx Zoo. The ever-changing story of Timmy led the local evening news in Cleveland. Radio shows discussed the brouhaha. Local newspaper editorials rehashed the particulars. Kate, the story went, had brought Timmy out of the emotional shell in which he'd been trapped since his capture in the jungles of Africa decades ago. In a way that no other female gorilla could—and there had been several previous females—Kate had healed a deep trauma in Timmy's life. The problem was, Kate was not making more gorillas. And so after much deliberation zoo officials finalized the paperwork: Timmy would, for the good of the species, be moved to New York. This decision only served to light bigger fires of concern, the epitome of which came in the form of a letter to the public claiming to have been a letter from Timmy himself. Eventually, the two sides landed in court. That the issue had gotten this far distressed zoo officials because it proved, obviously quite well, that the masses, out of their deep regard for animals, could come together and nearly topple a couple of heretofore well-established authorities on nonhumans: the Cleveland and the Bronx zoos.

I recount all this to show that there was, undoubtedly, an animal vibe in Cleveland at the time; and unless you were, say, under eight years old, the conflict, and the questions it raised, were inescapable. It was not so much, Could animals love? Could they feel? Could they experience longing?, though of course those things factored in. Instead, the overarching question was more an issue of humans having dominion over these gorillas, of our playing God in their lives, of our subduing and controlling their fate. Who, after all, were we to say that the ability of two gorillas to be fruitful, or not, should be the deciding factor in their lives? What was, or should be, our relationship to them? Granted, the talk was of gorillas, nonhumans very similar to humans. But it was not unthinkable that such ideas—since they were so consistently and heavily argued—could be debated about animals in general: the squirrels in Cleveland Heights, say, or the robins in Shaker Heights, the foxes and coyotes near Chagrin Falls.

Or red-tailed hawks in median strips of major highways, on any day, or on the Sunday I saw one, on my way to church. This came about because I had decided to forgo staying at a hotel while on assignment and to bunk, instead, with my friends C and M. And on this particular day, C, who was a Catholic feminist, asked M and me to attend a charismatic

Episcopalian liturgy at her church. . . . She assured M and me
that charismatic worship was a "gentle, healing, freeing, and
intimate way to expand one's relationship with God." . . .

We were talking cautiously, in the way friends must when
speaking of religion, when I glanced out the car window and
saw the red-tailed hawk in the median strip, mantling over, I
guessed, a field mouse just caught.

"Did you see that hawk!?" I interrupted. They had not,
and we kept driving.

At the Service

We arrived at the church, which looked like a large, contem-
porary white house on the outside and, inside, like the top
deck of a cruise liner, on the bow, where rows of chairs and
benches provide vacationers the opportunity to stare into the
flood of thought that oceans inspire. The simplicity of the interior, with several large beams running across the ceiling, reminded me of my vision of Noah's Ark, wherein Noah saved
animals no matter their state of cleanliness. His story, it
seemed to me, spoke through the power of metaphor to the
idea of preserving nonhumans regardless of their usefulness to
humans.

Before long, two hundred or so upper-middle-class parish-
ioners, fairly underdressed, gathered on the bow in small
groups to sip coffee, eat pastries, and discuss events of the
past week. There seemed not a frown in the place. After pat-
ting the cinnamon and sugar from our mouths and crumpling
our napkins, we took our seats across from a low stage that
had upon it the altar and a large cross. There were no stained-
glass windows, no flower arrangements, no dust, no incense,
no pews, no Bibles. I tried to remember that C had said it
would be this way, that there would be an ease here, an unfa-
miliar environment for the hard work of religion.

On our fold-up seats were photocopied pamphlets detail-
ing the morning's agenda, as well as a few pages of lyrics.

Three priests would manage the meeting, though Father Charles would lead. There would be the possibility, my neighbor whispered, that "people would be moved to speak in tongues or drop to the floor from the warmth of God's love entering their bodies." At other services, this woman continued, "people felt free enough to call out, to pray aloud, to soliloquize." This seemed fair; everyone would have the chance to be heard. During the next ninety minutes all these events did indeed occur. Though I admit to having snickered as discreetly as possible at the *Homo neanderthalensis*—like murmurings going on around me, and at the sudden falls to the carpet, I took the preaching seriously. For it was the preaching that, in the past, had been the bottleneck to believing.

What If God Is the Hawk?

Father Charles read and discussed several ideas before he began reading from Genesis: "And God said to them, Be fruitful and multiply, and replenish the earth, and subdue it: and have dominion over the fish of the sea, and over the fowl of the air, and over every living animal that moveth upon the earth."

This, I thought, might be a somewhat involved or messy passage for the day, given the state of things in Cleveland at the time. But there were no rebuttals in this court, no questions, no discussion. I wanted Father Charles to discuss the implications of moving, or not moving, beyond the typical interpretation of this passage, which is that of humankind as ruling master, and nature as slave. What, for instance, may have been lost in the translation from the Hebrew to English? And what might be the contributions of the expressions of the Psalms? Psalm 104: "You laid the earth's foundations so that they would never be destroyed. . . . May all selfishness disappear from me, and may you always shine from my heart." If Father Charles were to leap forward, to the New Testament, to the Resurrection, what could it mean that Jesus was mistakenly taken for a gardener? For was he not always a gardener and all that being a gardener implies, for humans as well as nonhumans: tending, replenishing, creating, and re-creating?

"Praise the Lord!" someone called out.

"Holy be the Lord!" another answered.

The passage apparently was accepted by citizens in a city that, at the time, was embroiled in questioning the human relationship to the nonhuman. Father Charles did not seize the opportunity to discuss the idea of preservation. He simply steered his ship through the same old waters, reminding me of a preacher Emerson described in *The Divinity School Address:* "He had no one word intimating that he had laughed or wept, . . . had been commended, or cheated, or chagrined. If he had ever lived and acted, we were none the wiser for it. The capital secret of his profession, namely, to convert life into truth, he had not learned."

Was this apparently fixed and unassailable thinking of Father Charles the crux of Nietzsche's concerns? Where was the wisdom of St. Augustine, the Christian theologian who said, "If you have understood, then this is not God. If you were able to understand, then you understood something else instead of God. If you were able to understand even partially, then you have deceived yourself with your own thoughts."

What if God *is* the hawk, *is* the fish of the ocean, the fowl of the air, and every living thing that moveth upon the earth? What if God *is* the grass the hawk sat in and the breeze the hawk flew through?

Off Being God

That I was a just a visitor to this church and unaccustomed in such environments to voicing questions—these should've been reasons to remain hushed and save my seat on the ship's bow. But I began feeling what I'd been warned I might: an unstoppable spirit and its concomitant urge to soliloquize oozing from my gut. It stumbled over my ribs, choked in my throat and loudly pushed through to Father Charles: *If you rule something, if you rule the earth, how can you love it!?* I yelled out.

Father Charles raised his hand toward me like a captain guarding a child running too close to the ship's safety rails: No walking beyond this point! Stop! And so this ark had sunk, and left me floating for a sense of the spiritual life.

Not long after, while everyone but C, M, and me was in line for communion, a woman bent down to me and, with a sudden and forceful hug, exclaimed, "Pray with us, honey!"

At the end of the service, just as we were heading for the door, a woman seized us and said, "Please come back. All your questions will be answered."

Since she was offering, I could not resist: "How," I said to her, hopefully, "would you answer my question?"

"The Lord knows best!" she said, breezing away, smiling.

Though C, M, and I knew that on our drive home the hawk would no longer be where it had been, we could not help looking for it out the window. Of course it was gone, somewhere, off being God.

Religion's Meaning

Most of the crowd around Majestic is gone. I walk toward her realizing that, prior to Cleveland, I arrogantly assumed that the environment could be saved with the panoply of laws and research available to scientists and the government. These were the educational, rational, logical tools I believed could be used to persuade people of the severe and urgent needs of the planet. But since Cleveland, I had floated to shore, so to speak; and without all the baptismal water in my eyes, it was clear that it would not take more science but a new kind of religion—Christianity reenvisioned, reimagined, reinvented—to supplant the idea that humans stand in a special relationship to God, separating and elevating us from all that is nonhuman.

So I walk toward Majestic as a spiritual gypsy, which is to say I go to her as the children went to Esther.

"May I touch her?" I ask her falconer. I want the privilege of skin against feathers.

"Sure, she loves to be touched," says the falconer.

I move my hand down her ivory-feathered chest, the source of her winged power, and stroke her clove-colored wings held tight against her body. She rouses slightly, stands tall, and tips her head back and to the right to look at the sky out of her left eye. When she turns her head back to the falconer, her gold eyes catch me for a second before she's on to more interesting things—sparrows in trees, other raptors around her, the dog trotting by. I can't seem to stop touching Majestic; and as long as she approves I continue devoting myself to this bird in a way that must look like childish fascination.

"To become fascinated is to step into a wild love affair on any level of life," Thomas Berry, the eminent cultural historian, once said. Is this feeling, this fascination, this devotion, this wonder, this love affair with a red-tailed hawk, a way to begin feeling religious again?

Religion. The origin of the word is from the Latin *religare,* meaning "to bind." Maybe religion is like a dog digging up its bones in the yard, coming to that which it loves and barking with rapture, with gratitude, for it. Perhaps religion continues through the ecstatic binding between the dog and his beloved object of devotion—between dog's paws and bone, between dog's teeth and bone, between dog's tongue and bone, between dog and his entire focus on bone, bone, bone.

Religion, you ask? Bark, with gratitude, like a dog. Call out like a heretic. Beg, and keep begging: "Please, please, I want to hold Esther!"

Developing Reverence for the Earth

Dennis Rivers

In this excerpt published by EarthLight Magazine, *peace activist and teacher Dennis Rivers argues that to mend the world and stop deforestation, animal extinction, wars, and environmental destruction, humans need to find new ways to revere and love Planet Earth. Rivers contends people must begin nourishing deep spiritual connections to one another and create loving relationships. Also, he writes that humans should embark on a path of devotion for nature and creation so intense that humanity's capacity to destroy will be restrained. Rivers edits several large peace and ecology Web sites, including newconversations.net and turntowardlife.org. He is also the editor of* Turning Toward Life, *an exploration of reverence for life as a spiritual path.*

Somewhere in his essays about the ecological crises of our time, I remember Wendell Berry [poet, farmer, and essayist from Kentucky] writing "What we do not love, we will not save." One of the many possible implications that I draw from his statement is that the eco-spiritual life is breath-like: the more we want to reach out to nurture the web of life (and save our own species along the way), the more deeply we will need to journey into our own hearts to connect with love's sustaining energy.

Although Planet Earth needs love the way a person lost in the desert needs water, love cannot be summoned by a simple act of will. Love, in my experience, is not like an object already in our possession, that we could give if we chose to do so. Love seems to me much more like a garden that will eventually bear fruit if cultivated in a spirit of apprenticeship, taking the time to learn about each tree and plant.

In this essay I will explore a five-fold vision of what might be called an ecology of devotion: a way of seeing how our various loves, concerns, gratitudes, adorations and celebrations are all part of a larger organic unity.

These many loves and concerns call to us, often in a chaotic din, urging us forward in many directions, appealing to us at many levels: friends need comfort, a new baby is born, the forests are dying, the dolphins are beaching, millions of landmines wait silently for human or animal footstep. Where and how shall we turn toward life and begin (or continue) the labors of "mending the world," the *Tikkun Olam* of Jewish tradition, which would also constitute the mending of our own broken hearts? As I have experienced the web of life being threatened by the explosive mix of greed, fear and technology, I have been challenged to find inside myself a love stronger than all fears, a deeper reverence for life that could be my compass through the chaos of a world unraveling.

Over the past year, in dialogue with a community of supportive friends called Turn Toward Life, I have been exploring a kind of mental rosary of our various loves and devotions, reverences that span the spectrum from gratitude to care to adoration. Like a garland with five flowers arranged in a circle, this five-fold rosary holds the various loves that struggle to be born in me. Here is how I see them, and how I will discuss them in the pages that follow:

> *reverence for the life that lives*
> *within us,*
>
> *reverence for the life that unfolds*
> *between us,*
>
> *reverence for the life that surrounds*
> *and sustains us,*
>
> *reverence for all the life of the fu-*
> *ture,*
>
> *reverence for the source of all life*

Reverence for the Life That Lives Within Us

The closest life for which we can have reverence is the life that lives within us, our breathing, moving, seeing, hearing, tasting, hoping, loving, yearning, and reaching; all the direct experiences of being alive, and those moments, often out in nature, when we suddenly feel good about being alive. I remember as a child the thrill, the infinite, bodily well-being, of running down a long beach near my house.

The Universe has labored mightily that we might breathe, and see the light of morning. The calcium, carbon and iron that support these processes were made in the hearts of ancient stars. The caloric energy that lets us run is compressed starlight, the light of the sun conveyed to us from leaf to corn and wheat through countless hands.

I have never felt more alive in my life than when I have been in love. For most of my life I took these feelings as revelations about the person with whom I was in love. Only in recent years have I begun to realize that these feelings were also saying something to me about my capacity to love, inviting me to get more acquainted with my own heart, with this intense aliveness. How is it that compressed starlight found this way of expressing itself? At times in my life I have complained bitterly to the Universe that love was not more evident in life. At some point the gestalt shifted and I suddenly realized how extraordinary it was that a universe composed mostly of rock and gas could have given birth to any experience of love, anywhere. And even more extraordinary was the fact that I was a carrier of this capacity, however clumsily I might carry it.

Our seemingly mundane existence, looked at from this angle, is a miracle of mind-boggling proportions. However ordinary or unworthy we may feel, we are nonetheless recipients of this galactic grace. Coming to understand how much we have received, beyond any measure of earning (for who could earn sunlight, or a billion years of evolution), sets the stage for us to give something back to life out of the fullness of gratitude, delight and awe. We are the Milky Way with arms and legs, eyes and ears, and hearts yearning to love. What will we create with the creative energy that the Universe has poured into us?

Reverence for the Life That Lives Between Us

There is a paradox at the heart of human unfolding: We can only love others to the degree that we are capable of loving ourselves. But, on the other hand, we are not born loving ourselves; we develop self-love by internalizing the love of all those who have loved us. As infants, we do not make our own food; neither do we make our own love.

Later in life, having been given the template, we may become bestowers of kindness; having been fed, we will feel the rightness of feeding others; having been nurtured by someone along the way, we will find a way to nurture others.

Like day and night, summer and winter, the nature that lives and breathes through us is full of polarities. I come into the fullness of MY personal being in relation to many YOUs. To cherish life at a deeper level is to accept this web of interwovenness, of land and sea, yes . . . of lake and forest, yes . . . but also, of *you* and *me*. This fragile human co-arising is as much a part of nature as spiderweb, wildebeeste or waterfall.

The life that emerges between us. . . . The partnership of bodies brings forth new bodies. The partnership of minds, brings forth new minds. Hearts joined in love invite everyone to love more. "Love one another," Jesus said, "as I have loved you," not only counseling his followers but also describing the path love travels down the generations, if we let it, because we let it. So also do hatred and oppression travel down the generations.

Loving the Earth Starts with Loving Each Other

And how beyond the circle of our human lives, one well might ask, is this related to ecology and reverence for life? In more ways than one would imagine. Perhaps the most dramatic link is that our human conflicts are having catastrophic impacts on other species. Driven by greed and unskilled in sharing, human beings are emptying the sea of fish and emptying the mountains of trees. Elephants in the jungles and forests of Indochina step on landmines just as people do. Our fears of our enemies, and their fears of us, have left the world awash in nuclear waste, which damages the gene-pools of human and animal alike. Ultimately, as Wendell Berry observes, we treat the natural world with the same love or disregard that we bestow on one another:

> The Earth is all we have in common. We cannot damage it without damaging those with whom we share it. There is an uncanny resemblance between our behavior with each other and our behavior toward the earth. The willingness to exploit one becomes the willingness to exploit the other. It is impossible to care for each other more or differently than we care for the earth.

To cherish the web of life, to protect life, it is now clear that we must necessarily face the shadow side of our own temperaments and our own cultures, the life that unfolds between us. For it is we humans, moved by various greeds and fears in relation to one another, who make and use these technologies of contamination and death.

The extremity of our predicament—that we are destroying our own life-support system as we drive many species over the brink of extinction—draws us toward the life that lives between us, not only as a source of despair, but also as a source of hope. Just as it is true that two together can carry a larger object than either would be able to carry alone, it is also true that in the company of supportive friends we can bear sorrows that are more than one heart can contain. I have become deeply convinced that creating an ecologically sustainable civilization will require creating a web of emotionally sustaining friendships, full of gratitude, listening and celebration. Gandhi would say start with yourself, be the change you want to see. A more intimate way of expressing this might be to say, embody the love, gratitude and compassion you want to promote.

Reverence for the Life That Surrounds and Sustains Us

This is the dimension of reverence for life that is most familiar to us, having been lived and expressed so beautifully by such eco-advocates as Albert Schweitzer, Rachel Carson, Jane Goodall, John Muir, Matthew Fox, Joanna Macy and Thomas Berry. Along with being great lovers of nature, these guiding lights were and are great students of nature.

A path of devotion in relation to the web of life around us is something more than just having a well of good feelings toward all creatures great and small, although that would be a great place to start. Feelings arise out of understandings. The more we understand about the history of each bite of food we take, the more likely we are to be filled with awe and gratitude. The more we know of fruit trees, the more each peach feels like a miracle. But if all of this is true, and the path toward a respectful partnership with the rest of nature is so straightforward, why is the world still falling apart. What is the problem? What follows is one approach to an answer.

Early in the twentieth century, the [Jewish] philosopher Martin Buber introduced what may be one of the most important distinctions in the history of human thought. Buber proposed that human beings do not have a sense of "I" in isolation. Rather, we have a sense of "I" in relation to someone or something. When we relate to another person as having experiences, feelings and purposes in the same way we do, we have an "I-Thou" sense of self. We strive to acknowledge the other person as an end in themselves, not merely as a means to the satisfaction of our own needs or desires. When we relate to an object that we experience as having no will, desire or consciousness of its own, we have an "I-It" sense of ourselves in relation to that object. We see the object as material for our use, as is often the case in relation to wood, food, oil, the ground that bears food, and members of ethnic groups other than our own. Buber acknowledged that we could not survive without using at least some of the objects in our world to sustain our lives. But he felt that we become truly human only when we are able to grant humanness to others, are able to feel others as worthy of our care and not just see others as sources of care, food, resources, power, status, etc. A healthy person would shift back and forth as appropriate, not treating a chair as if it were a person, but also not treating a person as if he or she were a chair.

The decades that followed the publication of Buber's book, *I and Thou*, developed the "I-Thou" and "I-It" ideas in two important ways. Within the field of human development, significant thinkers concluded that the ability to value other people as ends in themselves, distinct from oneself and yet worthy of care, was one of the central features of mature human development. And in the field of psychotherapy, there was a related realization that the inability to feel the personhood of others, as a consequence of severely disturbed early relationships, was one of the major character disorders of our era (including the "narcissistic personality"). People suffering from narcissistic personality disorder experience an inflated sense of entitlement in which everyone and everything are reduced to the status of furniture to be used at will. (Think of a mountain with all the trees cut down.)

Consequences of "I-It" Philosophy

I have given this extended introduction to Buber's ideas about the "I-Thou" and "I-It" ways of being a person because they describe the central area of problems for people in societies experiencing runaway industrialization. Runaway industrialization turns every person, plant and animal on Planet Earth into a heap of inert raw material, into psychologically dead stuff, all the better to plan for how it may all be used for the only source of purpose and value left in the world: profits in capitalist societies, the triumph of the state in totalitarian ones. This is the "I-It" sense of self writ large across the world, leaving behind a trail of clear-cut mountains and flooded lowlands. Capitalism, communism and totalitarianism agree deeply on one thing: living nature is really just dead stuff in motion, therefore we may do with it whatever we please.

The problem with this view is that, from a Buberian perspective, in "deadening" or depersonalizing the world in order to use it for our ends, we have deadened and depersonalized ourselves. We harden ourselves to not feel the pain of whomever and whatever we use, exploit and/or consume. And once having thus hardened, deadened and depersonalized ourselves, no amount of cars and refrigerators and 60-inch television sets can ever make us happy. We may not even feel the ecological cliff toward which we are racing.

In his book, *The Dream of the Earth,* [cultural historian] Thomas Berry describes how interwoven our personal development is with the web of life on Planet Earth. To grow up in a world that includes whales and tigers and elephants is to have evoked in oneself a very specific sense of beauty and majesty. When those creatures are gone, that specific sense will be gone, and the personhood of humanity will be radically diminished.

Seeing the no-win nature of the "I-It" path can be a shock, but can also free us to explore more sustainable and fulfilling ways of living. There are two sides to this realization: a warning and a promise. The warning is that whatever we inflict upon the world around us we inflict upon ourselves in a variety of ways. The promise, full of transformational possibilities, is also two-fold:

> the more value, beauty, depth of experience and purpose that we recognize and nurture in the world around us, the more of these we will be able to recognize and nurture in ourselves and in one another.

And the converse,

> the more value, beauty, depth of experience and purpose that we recognize and nurture in one another, the more of these we will be able to recognize and nurture in the larger web of life around us.

This suggests to me an almost-haiku:

start where you are the path is wherever you are standing

Reverence for All the Life of the Future

Like a pregnant woman big with child, the web of life today holds all future generations of life on Earth. Life blossoms forth through an endless spiral of eternal pregnancy, birthgiving, nurturing, coming together (of earth and seed, of egg and sperm) to begin again, and dying away to make way for the new.

Into this steady progression of ebbs and flows something new has entered, something that holds both promise and peril. In recent eras of evolution, *evolution itself has begun to evolve,* evolving from adaptation to adaptability, from the perfectly adapted claw to the hand and brain that can learn many new ways of holding many new things, and the evolution of a temperament to love one's offspring and teach them these new ways of holding.

We humans are not alone in this development; we share this evolution toward learning and creativity with many species, especially our primate brothers and sisters, chimpanzees, gorillas and baboons. And we are far from fully understanding of the intelligence of creatures quite different from us, such as dolphins and bee colonies. But we have gone further on this path of open adaptability, as far as we know, than any other species, and therefore our freedom and capacity to make catastrophic mistakes is much greater than that of any other species. No other creature, for example, leaves behind leaking piles of radioactive waste, slowly destroying the genetic integrity of all life as the radioactive contaminants circulate more and more widely through the biosphere.

Because we alone have developed the power to destroy all life, we alone are challenged to love all creatures intensely enough to want to save them, to love all creatures intensely enough to be willing to restrain our own appetites, to understand our own hatred and greeds. That, I submit to you, is a very intense devotion, a transformational gratitude, and, paradoxically, in this era of technological might, that all-embracing love has become the assignment of every human heart. As the cosmologist Brian Swimme has noted, from the point of view of species extinction our present era is the worst time in the last sixty-five million years. Without some deep transformation, it is not clear how life on Earth will continue. If there are going to be living plants and birds and fish and human beings in the future, it will be because we work to protect the seeds of their existence today, and the land and water that will make their lives possible. It will be because we open our hearts to love them now.

Reverence for the Source of All Life

In this exploration of reverence for life, I have deliberately shifted among a family of related words: love, reverence, devotion, gratitude, respect, service, celebration, nurture, protection, adoration. Other times and cultures would add such words as *agape, bhakti, karuna* and *caritas.* I used this wide variety of words out of my feeling that reverence for life is larger and more complex than any one word would suggest. I am deeply convinced, for example, that when we reach toward the source of all life, we are also reaching toward the ultimate source of love, because love is the core of our aliveness. In a fertile arc of self-referentiality, our capacity to love life is something that life itself is exploring and developing!

As children it is very difficult for us to imagine how we might have come out of our parents' bodies. Later we understand that, but struggle to bring into focus the way our personalities emerged from the matrix of personalities surrounding us when we were young. Eventually, we face the deepest mystery of all: how all of us, the family of life together, are continuously emerging out of the womb of an endlessly pregnant Universe. In the galactic unfolding of life, the life webs and planets that may survive are those who learn to love and nurture the ongoing miracle of their own co-emergence!

As our reverence for life deepens, it often deepens to include that something (or someone) larger than us, of which our lives are felt to be a creative and loving expression. The influence of science over the last few centuries has been to rule out such feelings of connectedness to something larger, because the science of that era could only look *down* the scale of connectedness at what were our "parts" and how those "parts" were hitched together. The emerging science looks both up and down and asks: what larger system enfolds this element (you and me), and how does this element function in relation to that larger system? Parts imply wholes, as your hand implies every bit of the rest of you, raising the extraordinary questions of what *we together* imply and what life implies.

Love Completes the Ecology of Devotion

We may never be able to fully grasp the larger system that enfolds us, but we have many hints and many suggestive analogies. Consider the fern in your garden. The tiniest part of a fern leaf bears the shape of the entire fern branch. When we turn to nature, we find that there are many such "fractal" examples, from trees to rivers to blood vessels, in which the very small mirrors the shape and function of the very large. So it is much more thinkable today than it was half a century ago, for us to feel that the noblest impulses in us express a larger nobility that enfolds us.

In my own life my sense of "the larger something of which I am a part" have been deeply influenced by the teaching, affirmed by many faiths using different vocabularies, that "God is love, and whoever dwells in love, dwells in God and God in them"—a truly fractal mysticism. For me, this teaching of lovingkindness, and the people who have embodied this lovingkindness, complete the spiral ecology of devotion.

I give thanks for the life that lives within me breath and heartbeat, joy and sorrow, dance and stillness

I give thanks for the life that lives between us as loving, understanding, creating, embracing and letting go

I give thanks for all the life forms that surround and support us for the web of life that feeds and protects us and also needs our care

I give thanks for all the life of the future hidden in the present moment and inviting us to walk the path of infinite, creative, compassion

I give thanks for the source of all life, and the source of my life, this living universe, of which my life is an expression.

CHAPTER 3

Environmental Ethics
and Justice

A Grandmother Fights for Clean Air and Water

Gregory Dicum

In this excerpt journalist Gregory Dicum tells the story of Marie Harrison, an environmental activist and grandmother fighting to close the Bayview-Hunters Point Power Plant located in her San Francisco community. Harrison was spurred to become an activist when her grandson and other neighborhood children began to suffer from various pulmonary problems and other ailments. She surmised that the emissions produced by the power plant were causing the illnesses, Dicum writes. After doing further research, Harrison learned that there are many leaking underground toxic sites in Bayview-Hunters Point. Harrison is now active with many organizations working to rid the community of dangerous pollution and waste. A freelance journalist for more than a decade, Gregory Dicum is a contributing editor at Other *magazine and writes a biweekly column for* SFGate, *the online edition of the* San Francisco Chronicle.

"I think Bayview-Hunters Point is one of the most beautiful places in the entire city," Marie Harrison told me when I visited her. "It is surrounded by water. It sits on a hill; it has a valley and greenery. The trees are now starting to blossom and grow."

Harrison may be the most optimistic person I have ever met. A lifelong resident of the downtrodden district, she knows all too well the harsh realities that come with living there.

"My grandson used to suffer tremendously," she told me, her eyes fixed steadily on my own. "He had asthma attacks and chronic nosebleeds. He would wake up some mornings with his pillow soaked with blood."

One particularly harrowing night in the hospital with him transformed Harrison into an environmental activist. She began to look outside her own family. "In the building where my grandson stays there were four units," she recalls. "Three of those units had children sick with asthma or another pulmonary disease. The other one had an adult with cancer, and the last one had an older child with really bad skin rashes. I thought, 'This is ridiculous.'"

"Up one more level,"—her grandson lived at the base of a hill—"three families out of the five in that unit had breathing problems. As I went up further, it got even worse. As you get to the top of the hill, you find babies who just got here having skin rashes and a hard time breathing. Babies! Good God almighty!"

A Grandmother's Fight Against Pollution

Lacking a background in public health but armed with an uncommonly forceful brand of common sense, Harrison quickly surmised that this cluster of suffering is caused by emissions from the Hunters Point Power Plant, which is directly across the street. Further research confirmed her suspicions.

"I became the biggest advocate for shutting down this power plant," says Harrison. "I told them, 'I have a vested interest in seeing this plant close. I will be after you. And if I lose, I'm coming back.'" She smiles. "I became the power plant's arch nemesis."

Harrison had been working in the community for decades, focusing on bringing in basic services other parts of the City might take for granted. Among her notable successes are an effort to bring a community college to Bayview-Hunters Point and the creation of a local credit union.

But her realization that night in the hospital made her shift her focus from what her community lacked to what it had in ghastly abundance: pollution.

"There are very close to 200 leaking underground toxic sites in Bayview-Hunters Point," Harrison tells me, beginning a catalog of horrors that would have the residents of any other San Francisco neighborhood up in arms. "There are two Superfund sites: the shipyard and the Bay Area Drum Co. There is the Hunters Point Power Plant and the Mirant Power Plant. There is the sewage-treatment plant."

These are some of the largest stationary sources of air pollution in the City, "and they're all in walking distance from one another—and I mean a leisurely walk," says Harrison. "And then there are the two freeways that intersect in Bayview-Hunters Point—101 and 280—another huge source of air pollution."

Pollution Inequity Impacts All Communities

Harrison's radicalization renewed her energy and put her at the forefront of the environmental-justice movement. The well-documented, almost intuitive idea that communities with less political power tend to be on the receiving end of the worst environmental problems was first enunciated in the late 1960s. By 1994, it had gained enough credibility that Bill Clinton issued an executive order to address the problem.

Yet, a decade later, little has changed.

A demoralized, poor, underrepresented and poorly educated community is the least equipped to fight for justice in a world of environmental-impact statements, epidemiological studies and litigation. Yet, for these same reasons, these communities are the least likely to get outside help. It's up to the communities themselves to make change happen. That's where Harrison comes in.

Her combination of community organizing and environmental activism has made her a potent force in Bayview-Hunters Point. She serves as a community organizer for Greenaction, an environmental advocacy group, is on the resident advisory board for the Hunters Point Naval Shipyard cleanup, serves on councils for the local community college, the community court and others and is a frequent contributor to *The San Francisco Bay View,* the area's newspaper. Her leadership and her example are beginning to transform the neighborhood. But her vision extends far beyond this locale.

"Bayview-Hunters Point is at ground zero," she explains. "The pollution we generate here walks the water all the way to Oakland and beyond if we get a good wind. You honestly think that what's happening in Bayview-Hunters Point is skipping the rest of the City? C'mon! Anything that happens to folks in Bayview-Hunters Point will happen to you."

Frustration Continues Despite Successes

Still, Harrison can get frustrated when people don't see the connections between their world and the life-and-death concerns of her neighborhood. "There are people in San Francisco who are more conscious of the environmental health of their pets than they are of the neighbor who lives across the street from them or around the corner, or on the opposite side of town. Not that a pet doesn't have that right, but don't you find there's something a little backward about it?"

As Harrison learned that her community is awash in pollution from systems whose benefits—power and plumbing, for example—are largely enjoyed elsewhere, she came to see that this situation bears all the hallmarks of latent racism. "San Franciscans are supposed to be the most liberal-minded folks in the whole world," she says, "but if we are it, then, oh, boy, is this world in trouble! And I say that not being disrespectful toward San Franciscans. They're not vicious or mean people— they really aren't. They just don't realize they are racist."

It's making that realization—and overcoming it—that lies at the heart of environmental justice in America. And there are signs that this process is starting to happen. Although it has been byzantine and sluggish and has moved at all due only to the persistence of people like Harrison, both the city government and PG&E now say they want the Hunters Point

Power Plant closed. (They maintain, however, that the state won't let them shut it down.)

At the end of last year [2004], however, Mayor Gavin Newsom announced the plant would close by 2007. But Harrison has learned from experience not to get her hopes up yet. She points out that the plant was originally scheduled to be shut down in 2001, and, for its neighbors, six more years of operation has meant six more years of poison and suffering. Together with Greenaction and 70 community members, Harrison blockaded the plant's gate in an effort to accelerate the closure.

The official—though disputed—reason for the plant's continued operation is to ensure that the City's power demands never go unmet, which implies that using electricity more efficiently may be one way to alleviate the need for the largest single point source of pollution in the City. "At one o'clock in the morning, why are the lights on at PG&E headquarters, down here on Beale Street?" Harrison asks incredulously. "Why is half of the Financial District lit up after folks have gone home? That's wasteful, and other folks are paying for this."

Yet, as tempting as it must seem after a life on the receiving end of endless industrial indignities, Harrison doesn't spread blame indiscriminately. "A lot of times, we cause harm and we don't realize it," she says. "A person who's going about their everyday business and really, truly does not realize that what they're doing is going to cause somebody harm is not truly guilty, I've learned to understand that."

Business Should Do No Harm

And this understanding extends to companies such as PG&E, Harrison adds. "They have a moral right to do their business, but it is also their moral responsibility to see to it that their businesses do no harm. So, when someone like me makes you aware that you're doing harm, it is your moral responsibility to do two things: one, find out if it's so—don't just take us at our word—and two, do something about it."

This, in the end, is why Harrison is such an optimist. She has faith that people will do the right thing once they know the truth, that together the City as a whole can clean up its act. "Those folks who are in charge need to know that it's not just some poor black folks over there in Bayview-Hunters Point," she says. "It's not about Bayview-Hunters Point—it's about San Francisco. If we're going to be the leaders that we're supposed to be—and everyone wants to believe that California and San Francisco really lead the way—then we need to step up to the plate and lead the way.

"People need to forget their differences—financial and class, or color, or religion," she adds, "and say, 'Those folks who live over in Bayview-Hunters Point have the same rights that we do.' They need to say it out loud and make sure that everyone around them knows that."

When Harrison speaks, her entire being is focused on her listener. Though she laughs freely—"I laugh because I have to," she tells me—her seriousness of purpose comes through as clearly as if she had just grabbed your shoulders and given you a good wake-up shake.

"We have the right to live, work, play and worship on land that is clean," Harrison says in no uncertain terms. "We have a right to breathe air that doesn't have all of the contaminants in it that our air does. Clean land and clean water and clean air is a God-given right. Environmental justice is the free access to that."

Private Property Must Be Protected from Extreme Environmentalists

Hillarie Brace

In 1987 the Environmental Protection Agency (EPA) ordered Pennsylvania farmer Robert Brace to stop farming thirty acres of his family's land because federal officials considered it wetlands. Brace had bought the land from his father in 1975 and, with funding from the U.S. Department of Agriculture, had installed a drainage system to improve the land so that he could plant crops. EPA officials, however, filed a lawsuit against him, contending that according to the federal Clean Water Act, it was not legal for Brace to use this drainage system because the acreage had been designated wetlands. Brace argued that his family had previously farmed the acreage, which he claimed did not have any standing water on it. The district court ruled against the EPA, stating that Brace's installation of the system constituted "normal farming practices." However, the Third Circuit Court of Appeals ruled in the EPA's favor, and the Supreme Court refused to hear the case. As a result Brace lost the right to farm his land and had to pay a $10,000 fine. In addition he has had to continue to pay property taxes on the unusable land. In 1998 Brace sued the government for compensation for the lost use of the land, which he claims is worth $3 million. In the summer of 2005 Brace was still waiting for a ruling from the U.S. Claims Court on his compensation case.

The following excerpt is from a speech by Brace's granddaughter, Hillarie Brace. Hillarie describes the impact the ongoing case has had on her family and urges others to educate themselves about environmental laws and the impact they can

Hillarie Brace, "Protect Your Property Rights! Take a Stand for Your Land!" www.pa landowners.org, March 5, 2005. Copyright © 2005 by the Pennsylvania Landowners Association. Reproduced by permission.

have on private property owners. She contends that citizens must protect the rights of private property to ensure the future of the nation.

I want to start off by asking you to take a second and think about your grandfather, or the general image of a grandfather. Now I'm sure you imagine the usual fishing trips, camping, backyard games, and warm hugs. Now let me tell you about my relationship with my grandfather. He has been fighting the government for his rights for almost 19 years. He is no different than any of your grandfathers; however he has been denied his rights guaranteed to him in the Fifth Amendment of the United States Constitution, and because of this he has not gotten to know his grandchildren like he should. We can thank the United States government for that. They showed up on his family farm in 1987 and told him he could no longer use a piece of his land, which, if put to its best use, would have an estimated value in excess of three million dollars. He did not only lose this profit, but was also forced to pay taxes and legal bills. This was all because the land fell under the category of "wetland." Now I understand the importance of wetlands and am not here to tell you that they aren't important; we need to realize, however, that as our government tries to protect the wetlands, they are ruining our nation. We need to educate everyone on this vital matter, before it is too late.

First, you have to realize how our government works. When you think of the government, you generally think of a system that helps the common good, all people. But if you believe that, you are mistaken. Yes I will agree that the government does help most people, however they do not help all of us. Slowly they are taking away our private property, making it public property, and destroying our nation. Picture this: you are fresh out of college, newly married, and are looking for somewhere to settle down. There is a beautiful one-hundred acre piece of land for sale with a price tag that fits your budget. The possibility remains, however, that the government will step in, once you have purchased it, and tell you that you must vacate it, return it to its natural state, and still pay taxes on it. You most likely are not going to purchase this land, correct? This threat does exist; however, most people are not aware of it. The government can step in at any time and take your land away, whether you think it is for a good reason or not. We need to educate everyone about this, especially those who are in high school, so that we may change this before it gets too far out of hand. If not we may find ourselves in that situation.

Environmental Laws Affect Everyone

Next, you need to realize that this does affect you.... No matter where you are at, you are mostly likely thinking about your future, myself included. Each and every one of us has high hopes it will be the very best. So why not start now to make these changes, so that they do not suddenly come upon us and startle us. When Bob Learzaf's uncle made a purchase of a parcel of land in 1923, he assumed, like anyone would, that he was guaranteed his rights by the Fifth Amendment and the land would remain rightfully his and in his family unless he sold it. This is not the case. In 1996, Bob was now the owner of the land, and he was told that he must vacate the property and burn his cabin.[1] We need to get the word out about situations like this and educate ourselves so that we don't become victims like Learzaf.

Educate Yourself About Environmental Extremism

Lastly, I would like to bring to your attention that all of us are environmentalists to some extent. We all have probably recycled something at one point in our lives, picked up a piece

1. In 1996 the U.S. Forest Service ordered Bob Learzaf to vacate his property and cabin in Pennsylvania, claiming that his land belonged to the government and that Learzaf's original bill of sale was invalid. Learzaf refused to give up his land, and in 2000 was sentenced to one year's probation and fined $2,000. The government also took possession of the land.

of discarded trash, and all want a clean environment in which to live. There are those extreme environmentalists, however, which pose a threat to our property. [President of the Endangered Species Coalition] Brock Evans is one of these extreme environmentalists, of private property he says, "Let's take it all back." Extreme environmentalists believe that we do not actually own land, they believe that we are just here for a short period of time to care for the land, then we die and someone else takes over that duty. Now I agree that we are only here for a short time and that once we pass away, someone else will take over our duties. I do not believe, however, that we do not own land. We pay a purchase price, taxes, and other fees to maintain the land. Extreme environmentalists, with their attitude towards the whole thing, however, will do whatever it takes to deprive an individual of their private property. Even a piece of seemingly dry land may be considered wetlands if the choice of classification falls into the wrong hands. If we educate ourselves ... we will have a much better chance at protecting ourselves from facing this horrible situation.

In conclusion, I am asking you to educate yourself and those around you about property rights. This way, when you purchase your property, you will not be denied the rights guaranteed to you by the Fifth Amendment of the United States Constitution, and your land will remain your own.

Saving the Yellowstone Wolf

Hank Fischer

The Yellowstone wolf is making a major comeback in the western United States, thanks to an incentive program funded by the Defenders of Wildlife, a nonprofit conservation organization with more than 490,000 members and supporters. In this excerpt wildlife biologist and journalist Hank Fischer details how the program began in 1987. He writes that by 2001 the program helped to reintroduce more than four hundred wolves into Yellowstone National Park and central Idaho. The program's main goal is to win support from ranchers for the reintroduction program by compensating ranchers who suffer loss of livestock to wolves. Fischer has been involved in a variety of public land issues. Previously the project director for the Wildlife Defenders' publication, Building Economic Incentives into the Endangered Species Act, *Fischer now works for the National Wildlife Federation as a manager for the Wildlife Conflict Resolution program.*

I confess to having no greater affection for wolves than for any other creature. I don't wear a wolf hat, I don't collect wolf pictures, and I don't even own a wolf coffee mug. My passion is with Yellowstone's natural system as a whole. I'm captivated by the intricate interplay of wolves with elk, aspen, beetles, ravens, fire, weather, and people—the part of the equation often overlooked. All these parts, plus thousands we've yet to understand, working together in a random yet reciprocal way, create the wildness that we know as Yellowstone.

Modern ecologists suggest that the large predators "are the big things that run the world." They create changes that ripple through the entire system, affecting everything from elk down to the smallest clump of bluebunch wheatgrass. I want to help restore a place in North America where we have as full a complement of an ecosystem as we can have, something to measure other ecosystems against. We are beginning to have that in the greater Yellowstone region.

Incentives are critical to wolf conservation. My first insight into their importance came in a small schoolhouse in St. Anthony, Idaho, in 1984. I had brought together about twenty livestock producers from the area who would be affected by reintroduction of wolves. I thought that if I could better understand their concerns, together we could figure out what we needed to do to bring wolves back to Yellowstone National Park and central Idaho.

Confrontation by Ranchers

As I entered that schoolhouse, I was confronted by a sea of cowboy hats. I immediately recognized one old sheep rancher I had previously had some run-ins with over predator control issues. As I started my talk he stood up and bellowed, "Hank Fischer, you mean nobody's kilt you yet?" Actually, he was trying to be friendly, but the humor reveals how tense everybody was.

I explained to the ranchers that wolves aren't like grizzlies. They have a high reproductive rate; they're not attracted to humans; and livestock losses to wolves are not very high. A rancher stood up and said, "It's easy to be a wolf lover. It doesn't cost anything. It's the people who own livestock who end up paying for wolves." I explained to him that in Minnesota the state offers a compensation program, and that perhaps such a program could be developed in Idaho and Montana. His response: "Hope is a good breakfast but it's a mighty poor supper." As I closed up the meeting, one of the final questions was, "What's the best caliber to shoot a wolf with, anyway?"

The ranchers may not have learned much from me, but I picked up a few things. Foremost, I learned that I didn't have

In an attempt to save and reintroduce the wolf population back into Yellowstone, conservationists are offering to pay ranchers for livestock killed by wolves. © William Campbell/ Sygma/CORBIS

a good answer for their most central question: why should they have to pay the costs of wolf introduction?

About a year later Defenders of Wildlife sponsored an exhibit about wolves that traveled around the country. At the time, it was the largest wildlife exhibit ever constructed. Its purpose was to get people to examine how they felt about wolves and why. Defenders decided to bring the exhibit to Yellowstone Park to get the public and the Park Service thinking about Yellowstone wolf restoration.

That was when I had a chance to talk to William Penn Mott, Ronald Reagan's National Park Service director. He seemed to speak off the top of his head, but he offered me the most farsighted piece of wolf wisdom anyone has ever given me. He said, "The single most important action that conservation groups could take to advance Yellowstone wolf restoration would be to start a compensation fund. It's economics that makes ranchers hate wolves. Pay them for their losses and the controversy will subside."

Using Compensation to Solve Rancher/Wolf Conflict

In 1987, wolves were returning naturally to northwestern Montana (near Glacier National Park), and that summer wolves killed livestock east of Browning. The ranchers lost several thousand dollars' worth of livestock, and they were angry. The issue was in the newspapers for months. Given this anger, I had to think about how we could put a better face on wolf restoration.

The only solution was to pay these ranchers for their losses. I sent a fund-raising letter to several Defenders of Wildlife members in Montana, and I had the necessary funds within 48 hours. We paid about $3,500 to those ranchers. Suddenly, the wolf/livestock conflict was no longer an issue dominating the newspapers. It disappeared. I went back to my organization and said, "Let's keep doing this."

To raise money, Montana artist Monte Dolack created his vision of how wolves might look if restored to Yellowstone Park. We sold posters of this artwork for $30 each and raised over $50,000. We were on our way to a permanent program.

Since 1987, when we made the first payment in Browning, we have paid approximately $175,000 to ranchers for wolf compensation. The program covers Montana, Idaho, Wyoming, Arizona, and New Mexico. In 1997 Defenders initiated a grizzly bear compensation program for Montana and Idaho (Wyoming has its own state program). That program has paid over $60,000 for livestock losses caused by bears.

Keeping the Program Simple

We try to make these programs as simple as possible, and we do not require the ranchers to do any paperwork. We rely on state or federal agencies to verify the losses. When I learn about a probable wolf kill, I typically call the livestock producer and talk with him or her. These are important conversations, a half-hour to an hour long. I want the ranchers to tell what happened as they see it. Through these conversations I'm trying to bridge the gap between people who may not want wolves and my organization, which is committed to wolf restoration.

Many ranchers tell me, "I don't mind having wolves around, but I can't afford to have them killing my livestock." In a sense, we are attempting to make a contract. Our side of the contract is that wolves that kill livestock will be controlled (moved, relocated, or killed). Their side of the contract is to tolerate wolves that do not kill livestock.

Livestock producers have made important suggestions that have allowed us to improve our compensation program. For example, an animal killed in March or April—say, a young lamb—has a low market value. But the owner has made an investment based on the value of the sheep that will go to market in the fall. So we compensate ranchers not at current market value, but at the fall value of their livestock.

Another issue was how to handle situations where it appeared likely that wolves killed livestock, yet it couldn't be determined for certain. To deal with this gray area, we set up a category we call "probable" losses. In such situations we compensate at fifty percent of market value instead of full market value.

Since the reintroduction program began in 1995, the number of wolves in the wild in Yellowstone and central Idaho has gone from zero to over four hundred animals. Currently there are thirteen wolf packs in Yellowstone.

Wolves Are Here to Stay

It's time to move past the stage of conflict. Many people on both sides are still fighting. Some ranchers still argue that wolves should never have been reintroduced in the first place, and some environmentalists still argue that government protections for wolves are too weak. Both ignore the reality that wolves are now present in healthy numbers and are here to stay.

The important issue now is how broadly wolves will be distributed across the West. Currently wolves are limited primarily to national parks and wilderness areas. If wolves are to recolonize other areas, people may need to make changes in their livestock operations. The issue once again revolves around economics: who should pay for these changes?

My view is that people who support wolf recovery should help pay the costs. Last year [2000] Defenders created a new Proactive Carnivore Conservation Fund. This fund supports collaborative projects that we develop with livestock producers designed to prevent wolf and grizzly predation on livestock from occurring in the first place. It might involve sharing the cost of constructing a secure night pasture for sheep, it might involve "bear-proofing" garbage dumpsters, or it might involve constructing an electric fence around beehives. Or if wolves were denning in a pasture normally used by livestock, Defenders might share the cost of finding alternate pasture. When people start working together, we find that there are many ways for wolves and livestock grazing to coexist.

At the same time, there may be situations where we have paid compensation and taken proactive measures to avoid predation, yet predator/livestock conflicts remain. Some areas are so attractive to large carnivores that it may be hard to keep them away. The solution may be to offer ranchers an incentive to shift to a different location. If they are having constant problems with grizzlies on their grazing allotment, it might be in the ranchers' interest as well to move to a new location.

In sum, the people who support wolves need to take economic responsibility for them. But this program is about a lot more than money. It's about respecting what the ranchers do. Eventually, I want wolves to be just another animal, not up on a pedestal as they are now. I want to get past the point where they are such a big deal. I want them to be an important part of a large and healthy ecosystem.

SOCIAL ISSUES
FIRSTHAND

CHAPTER 4

Environmental Activism

A Personal Commitment to Animals and the Earth

Marc Bekoff

In this excerpt from the book The Ten Trusts: What We Must Do to Care for the Animals We Love *by Marc Bekoff and Jane Goodall, Bekoff summarizes the reasons people need to work together to save animals and their habitats. He argues that humans and animals are interconnected and need each other to ensure survival. He also encourages people to take small steps toward environmental conservation by recycling and reducing the amount of energy they consume. Bekoff writes that it is everyone's responsibility to live in harmony with Earth. A University of Colorado biology professor, Marc Bekoff has written many books on animal behavior and conservation. Bekoff is a regional coordinator for the Roots & Shoots program. Founded by renowned chimpanzee researcher and conservationist Jane Goodall, the program promotes environmental awareness and community involvement for young people, senior citizens, and prisoners in over seventy countries.*

I live in the mountains outside of Boulder. I love where I live because I am a "biophiliac"—a lover of all nature—at heart. A few years ago I had a window installed that allows me to look at a magnificent ponderosa pine tree. When I asked my friend to do the carpentry, he was incredulous—"You'll just see the darned tree," he told me. As if I didn't know! "I know," I told him, "I love trees! I can see mountains from other windows, but seeing and feeling the presence of this tree makes me feel good—makes me smile—makes me appreciate all of nature." Often I just sit and stare at "tree" and wonder what it is feeling.

Trees are wonderful beings, and they provide all sorts of comfort for many animals. They are sought as homes and refuges, but . . . refuges are not always safe havens. . . . [Renowned animal researcher] Jane [Goodall] tells of the horror of seeing a treed cougar shot in Wyoming. Because I've also chosen to live among cougars, I've had a number of close encounters with them. Once, on a very dark and starry night, I got out of my car to say hello to my neighbor's German shepherd, Lolo, only to realize when I heard Lolo barking behind me that I was saying hello to a large male cougar who had just killed a red fox below my house! A few years ago I almost stepped on a cougar as I walked backward down my road, telling my neighbor that there was a cougar in the neighborhood and that he should watch his kids and his dog! Since then, I've merely changed my ways so that I can coexist with the magnificent beasts—cougars, black bears, coyotes, red foxes, deer, and many species of birds and insects—who have allowed me to move into their neighborhood. I now hike with my canine companion, Jethro, carrying bear spray and a flashlight; often I put a flashing red light and a bell on Jethro's collar—simple adjustments indeed.

Let us not forget that in most instances we have intruded on other animals—they are not the intruders. And many animals suffer each and every day because of the messes we make. In a sense Earth is part of an uncontrolled "experiment" in which each of us plays a part. In May 2001, Jane and I were sitting at an outdoor cafe in Paris, France (at a meeting of the group Science and the Spiritual Quest II), when we saw a pigeon hobbling along, one of her legs wrapped in a piece of wire. We tried to catch her, but she evaded us. There was nothing we could do but lament this poor bird's plight. Birds also get their heads stuck in plastic bottle carriers, and other animals often suffer from trash left behind at campsites and in oceans, rivers, and lakes. Not only are humans all over the place, but so is our trash. Many of us, but surely not all of us, simply have too much "stuff."

We Are Not Alone

We are not alone on this planet, although we frequently behave as if we were. Our big old slowly evolving brains that are confronted by new and rapidly evolving sociocultural milieus not only keep us somewhat in contact with nature but also remove us from nature, and this alienation results in our wanton abuse of the Earth. We are continually faced with making difficult and oftentimes agonizing choices that have short-term and long-term consequences. And we must look at the overall effects of our activities. Our influence is not always evident even in the short-term. For example, global warming appears to be having an impact on the number of primates living in Ethiopia. A rise in temperature leads to less grass and fewer crops on which gelada baboons are able to graze, and it is feared that their numbers will fall because of this. In addition to causing decreased numbers of gelada baboons, drought also reduces play among juveniles, and the lack of play in youngsters may have large effects on the social behavior and social organizations of adults.

In addition to a wide variety of mammals, birds also suffer from climatic warming and the recession northward of the polar ice pack. Long-term studies are needed to show the effects of climate change. [Arctic biologist] George Divoky's three decades of research on Cooper Island in the Arctic has shown that pigeon-sized seabirds, black guillemots, have suffered because as the ice edge moves offshore and retreats northward, individuals are unable to reach the ice edge and consequently die. The extent of ice in the Arctic Ocean decreased 3 percent per decade between 1978 and 1996, and the sea ice in the Nordic seas has decreased about 30 percent during the past 130 years. It has been predicted that summer ice in the Arctic Ocean might shrink as much as 60 percent as carbon dioxide doubles.

The abuse and killing of animals continues, but we must make our objections known. Given what some people choose to do to animals, I often wish they were not the marvelous and magical beings they are. But the fact is that many animals do indeed suffer brutal exploitation and intense pain, and we must change our ways—now. We need animals and love animals because they are feeling beings, not because they are unfeeling "things." Of course, even animals who might not be able to experience pain and suffering deserve our respect and consideration so that their lives are not compromised by our self-centered activities. We do not have to be afraid of being sentimentalists or apologize for our idealism. Perhaps it seems to no avail at the moment, but as more and more people object to animal abuse and the exploitation of our environment, our children all will reap the benefits. We must remain hopeful that a universal ethic of courage, caring, sharing, respect, radical compassion, and love will make a difference even if we do not see the positive results of our efforts. Frustrations and personal insults need to be pushed aside, for tangible rewards do not frequently immediately follow activism for animals and the Earth.

Every Individual Can Make a Difference

We must also deeply believe that the voice and the actions of every individual also make a difference, for they do. Martin Luther King, Jr., once said: "A time comes when silence is betrayal." He was right—silence and indifference can be deadly for our animal friends and for the Earth.

There is an old saying: "After all is said and done, much more's been said than done." Although this is so for our interactions with animals, the human community, and the Earth . . . , we have indeed made much progress in making this a better world, a more compassionate world in which caring and sharing abound. By "minding animals" and "minding the

Earth" numerous animals, people, and habitats are far better off than they would have been in the absence of an ethic blending together respect, caring compassion, humility, grace, and love. Caring about some being or some thing, any being or any thing, can spill over into caring for everybody and everything. If we focus on the awe and mystery of other animals and the Earth, perhaps we will be less likely to destroy them.

Allowing ourselves to sense the presence of other animals, to feel their residence in our hearts, brings much joy and peace and can foster spiritual development and a sense of unity. And this happiness, this sense of bliss, allows for Earth, bodies of water, air, animals, and people to be blended into a seamless tapestry, a warm blanket of caring and compassion, in which every single individual counts and every single individual makes a difference. The interconnectedness of individuals in a community means that what one does affects all—what happens in New York influences what happens across the world in Beijing and other distant locales.

Our Interconnectedness Exemplified

Recently I read a report that emphasized just how interconnected we all are. Scientists from the U.S. Geological Survey discovered that dust from the Sahara Desert is blown across the Atlantic Ocean and found in the Caribbean and in the United States. This dust carries with it tiny microbes that survive the five-to-seven-day journey. Bacteria, fungi, and viruses actually hitch a ride across the ocean and find their way to locations thousands of miles away. As a result, there is a heightened risk of respiratory diseases. One study found that on a dusty day there was an average of 158 bacteria and 213 viruses in a quart of air, whereas on a clear day there was an average of only 18 bacteria and 18 viruses in the same volume of air.

Back in 1963, President John F. Kennedy spoke the following words, which still apply today: "For in the final analysis, our most basic common link is that we all inhabit this small planet. We all breathe the same air. We all cherish our children's future. And we are all mortal." We are the community of Earth—we only have one Earth—and we need community now more than ever.

As I am writing this brief conclusion and getting weary—long days, horrible animal abuse here and there, incessant environmental damage due to human activities—I am rekindled when I receive an e-mail telling me of a team of more than two hundred Nahua Indian women in the Mexican state of Puebla who are involved in a wonderful environmental program that involves running a hotel and managing a health-food store, a greenhouse for medicinal plants, and a crafts store in which they produce recyclable paper and biodegradable cleaning products. And the good news continues. In May 2002 Germany became the first European country to vote to guarantee constitutional rights to animals. And Mexico became the world's largest national whale sanctuary when it signed an accord to protect whales in its waters, an area of about 1.1 million square miles. And in India, the newly founded National Institute of Animal Welfare now offers a B.A. degree in animal welfare. A Japanese fisherman recently refused to kill dolphins because "they cry when they are about to die . . . I cannot kill something when tears are rolling down its cheeks." In surveys of more than 1,500 people in Europe and the United States, 70 to 90 percent of the respondents "recognize the right of nature to exist even if not useful to humans in any way." . . .

And there is Zivvy Epstein, who loves rain forests and wants to spend his life trying to save them. Zivvy is part of the Roots & Shoots program that I helped to organize with Addie Rocchio and Stacey Selcho at the Collage Children's Museum in Boulder. At his seventh birthday party Zivvy collected $442 rather than gifts and gave this money to the Rainforest Alliance. . . .

Let Us Be Ethicists, Not Ostriches

As a child of the sixties, I am a dreamer with few bounds. I ask the people with whom I interact to imagine that they carry a suitcase of courage, compassion, and hope and that because they receive what they give, the supply of courage, compassion, and hope will never be exhausted. It is easy to have one's spirit and soul weathered by the "bad" things that happen around us. It seems as if we are addicted to the destruction of the very animals and landscapes we love. But many, many good things are happening each and every day all over the world that can kindle our spirit and impel us to act.

Jane and I hope that we have inspired you to act—to do something, anything—to make this a better world. As [anthropologist] Margaret Mead noted: "Never doubt that a small group of thoughtful, committed citizens can change the world. Indeed, it is the only thing that ever has." It is important to focus your efforts and not be deflected by those who oppose you. It's a waste of time and energy to "fight" your opponents who only gain when you divert your attention to them rather than to the important issues at hand. It is never too late to do something. Even if you have only one minute, or ten seconds a day, you can make a difference. Talk to friends and families while taking a break, while taking a walk, while just "hanging out." Shut off lights, take shorter showers, walk rather than drive, recycle, or say "hello" to a passerby. Write letters to local media. The small fraction that we each offer can contribute to larger solutions. Even a tiny ripple—a little agitation—can spread widely and rapidly. Even if you have time to help only one individual, you can make a difference. It is thought that North Atlantic right whales might survive if only one or a few females are spared each year—one whale counts.

And be resourceful. Use a blend of scientific data, common sense, and anecdotes to assess information and to make choices about what to do in a given situation. In this high-tech world there are innumerable sources available almost instantaneously. Jane told me about an introduced plant that was overtaking Buffalo, New York, but could not remember its name. I called a bed and breakfast establishment in Buffalo, figuring that those in the tourism business might know about some of the local ecological problems, and they did! I learned that it was the purple loosestrife . . . , and that many people are indeed concerned about this nasty invasive plant that is rampantly taking over native plants in many regions. My sense of despair was replaced with a sense of hope. I think some people get discouraged and lose hope because they do not have the facts, and after talking to some of my colleagues about this and other problems that I thought were thoroughly unsolvable, I discovered that they could be dealt with if people knew what was really happening. And when we are unsure, I favor erring on the side of animals and nature.

The innumerable problems that currently exist will not disappear if we bury our heads in the sand like ostriches. The situation will only get worse. Achieving win-win situations for all humans and animals (and other nature) in the labyrinth of conflict and confusion will be very difficult, but we should never stop trying. If we fail to do so, I fear that we, our children and theirs, other animals, and nature as a whole will lose, and that much of the spark, spirit, and soul that keeps us going in our attempts to make this a better world will be extinguished. Fortunately, it is my impression, and others agree, that more students and people in general are now interested in ethical issues than had previously been the case, and that there is a progressive trend toward caring more and doing more, not less, for animals, people, and the Earth. I am amazed and thrilled that a search on the Worldwide Web for "animal protection," "conservation," or "biodiversity" produces tens of thousands of "hits."

Answering the Challenging Environmental Questions

Do we really want to live in harmony with nature? Are we

truly the people we think we are? These are simple yet extremely challenging questions. If we answer yes to either or both, which not only is politically correct but also ethically and ecologically correct, we are compelled to move forward with grace, humility, respect, compassion, and love. We will need to replace "mindlessness" with "mindfulness" about our interactions with animals and the Earth. Nothing will be lost and much will be gained. We can never be too generous or too kind.

Surely, we will come to feel better about ourselves if we know deep in our hearts that we did the best we could and took into account the well-being of the magnificent animals with whom we share Earth, the awesome and magical beings who selflessly make our lives richer, more challenging, and more enjoyable than they would be in the animals' absence. Doesn't it feel good to know that there are animals "out there" whom we have helped even if we cannot see them? Doesn't it feel good to know that we did something to help the Earth even if we do not see the fruits of our labor? As we attempt to restore nature, we can restore ourselves, our psyches that have been fragmented because of our alienation from animals and other nature. We often turn toward nature when we're feeling down. We need animals, nature, and wildness. . . .

Let us never avert our eyes from the gaze of the animals who need us and whom we need as much or more. Life without our animal friends would be lonely and miserable. In the grand scheme of things, individuals receive what they give. If love is poured out in abundance, then it will be returned in abundance. There is no need to fear depleting the potent and self-reinforcing feeling of love that continuously can serve as a powerful stimulant for generating compassion, respect, and more love for all life. Each and every individual plays an essential role and that individual's spirit and love are intertwined with the spirit and love of others. These emergent interrelationships transcending individuals foster a sense of oneness. These interrelationships can work in harmony to make this a better and more compassionate world for all beings. We must stroll with our kin and not leave them in the wake of our tumultuous, rampant, self-serving destruction.

By minding animals we mind ourselves. Personal transformations are needed and will serve us well. We owe it to future generations to transcend the present, to share dreams for a better world, to step lightly, to move cautiously with restraint. We destroy one another when we destroy the Earth. We all can be dreamers and doers. We owe it to ourselves and to other animals, to whom we can, unfortunately, do whatever we choose. We owe it to ourselves to keep in mind the power of love. As big-brained, omnipresent, powerful, and supposedly omniscient mammals, we are the most powerful beings on Earth. We really are that powerful, and with that might are inextricably tied innumerable staggering responsibilities to be ethical human beings. We can be no less.

We Need to Cut Down Trees to Save the Environment

Patrick Moore

In this excerpt Patrick Moore, a founding member of Green-peace, argues that cutting down trees and using more wood is the answer to the world's environmental problems. Moore writes that environmentalists misrepresent the forestry industry as the main cause of species extinction. Instead, he argues, forestry is the most sustainable of all the primary industries because wood is a renewable energy. He contends that the environmentalists' push to use less wood and to cut down fewer trees is an antienvironmental policy because to replace wood, humans would have to use more nonrenewable products such as plastics, steel, and cement. Factories that rely on heavy use of fossil fuels produce these products. The result, he writes, would be an increase in carbon dioxide emissions, leading to more ozone depletion and drastic climate changes. Moore is an internationally renowned ecologist and environmentalist who began his career as an activist and leader in the Greenpeace movement. After leaving Green-peace in 1990 Moore founded Greenspirit, an organization focusing on consensus building in environmental policy development.

I believe that trees are the answer to a lot of questions about our future. These include: How can we advance to a more sustainable economy based on renewable fuels and materials? How can we improve literacy and sanitation in developing countries while reversing deforestation and protecting wildlife at the same time? How can we pull carbon out of the atmosphere and reduce the amount of greenhouse gases emissions, carbon dioxide in particular? How can we increase the amount of land that will support a greater diversity of species? How can we help prevent soil erosion and provide clean air and water? How can we make this world more beautiful and green? The answer is, by growing more trees and then using more wood, both as a substitute for non-renewable fossil fuels and materials such as steel, concrete and plastic, and as paper products for printing, packaging and sanitation.

The forest industry stands accused of some very serious crimes against the environment. It is charged with the extinction of tens of thousands of species, the deforestation of vast areas of the Earth, and the total and irreversible destruction of the ecosystem. If I were one of the urban majority, and I thought the forest industry was causing the irreversible destruction of the environment I wouldn't care how many jobs it created or how many communities depended on it, I would be against it.

Environmentalism Background

I have spent the last 15 years trying to understand the relationship between forestry and the environment, to separate fact from fiction, myth from reality. Since 1991 I have chaired the Sustainable Forestry Committee of the Forest Alliance of British Columbia. This has provided an ideal opportunity to explore all aspects of the subject. This presentation is the synthesis of what I have learned. But first, let me give you a little background.

I was born and raised in the tiny fishing and logging village of Winter Harbour on the northwest tip of Vancouver Island, in the rainforest by the Pacific. I didn't realize what a blessed childhood I'd had, playing on the tidal flats by the salmon spawning streams in the rainforest, until I was shipped away to boarding school in Vancouver at age fourteen. I eventually attended the University of BC [British Columbia] studying the life sciences: biology, forestry, genetics; but it was when I discovered ecology that I realized that through science I could gain an insight into the mystery of the rainforest I had known as a child. I became a born-again ecologist, and in the late 1960's, was soon transformed into a radical environmental activist. I found myself in a church basement in Vancouver with a like-minded group of people, planning a protest campaign against US hydrogen bomb testing in Alaska. We proved that a somewhat rag-tag looking group of activists could sail a leaky old halibut boat across the north Pacific ocean and change the course of history. By creating a focal point for opposition to the tests we got on national TV news in Canada and the US, building a ground swell of opposition to nuclear testing in both countries. When that bomb went off in November 1971 it was the last hydrogen bomb ever detonated on planet Earth. Even though there were four more tests planned in the series, President Nixon canceled them due to the public opposition. This was the birth of Greenpeace.

Flushed with victory and knowing we could bring about change by getting up and doing something, we were welcomed into the longhouse of the Kwakiutl Nation at Alert Bay near the north end of Vancouver Island where we were made brothers of the tribe because they believed in what we were doing. This began the tradition of the Warriors of the Rainbow, after a Cree legend that said that one day when the skies are black and the birds fall dead to the ground and the rivers are poisoned, people of all races, colors and creeds will join together to form the Warriors of the Rainbow to save the Earth from environmental destruction. We named our ship the Rainbow Warrior and I spent fifteen years on the front lines of the eco-movement as we evolved from that church basement into the world's largest environmental activist organization [Greenpeace]. . . .

Changing from Confrontation to Consensus Building

By the mid-1980's Greenpeace had grown from that church basement to an organization with an income of over US$100 million per year, offices in 21 countries and over 100 campaigns around the world, now tackling toxic waste, acid rain, uranium mining and drift net fishing as well as the original issues. We had won over a majority of the public in the industrialized democracies. Presidents and prime ministers were talking about the environment on a daily basis.

For me it was time to make a change. I had been against at least three or four things every day of my life for 15 years; I decided I'd like to be in favor of something for a change. I made the transition from the politics of confrontation to the politics of building consensus. After all, when a majority of people decide they agree with you it is probably time to stop hitting them over the head with a stick and sit down and talk to them about finding solutions to our environmental problems. . . .

Coming from British Columbia, born into a third generation forest industry family, and educated in forestry and ecology, it made sense that I would focus on the challenge of defining sustainable forestry. After all, forests are by far the most important environment in British Columbia and they are also by far the most important basis of economic wealth for families and communities. . . .

Forests are home to the majority of living species; not the oceans, nor the grasslands, nor the alpine areas, but ecosystems that are dominated by trees. . . .

Environmentalist Propaganda

This gives rise to the obvious concern that if the trees are cut down the habitats or homes will be lost and the species that live in them will die. Indeed, in 1996 the World Wildlife Fund, at a media conference in Geneva, announced that 50,000 species are going extinct each year due to human activity. And the main cause of these 50,000 extinctions, they said, is commercial logging. The story was carried around the world by Associated Press and other media and hundreds of millions of people came to believe that forestry is the main cause of species extinction.

During the past three years I have asked the World Wildlife Fund on many occasions to please provide me with a list of some of the species that have supposedly become extinct due to logging. They have not offered up a single example as evidence. In fact, to the best of our scientific knowledge, no species has become extinct in North America due to forestry.

Where are these 50,000 species that are said to be going extinct each year? They are in a computer model in [professor and biologist] Edward O. Wilson's laboratory at Harvard University. They are electrons on a hard drive, they have no Latin names, and they are in no way related to any direct field observations in any forest. . . .

The spotted owl is one of the many species that was never threatened with extinction due to forestry, and yet in the early 1990's, 30,000 loggers were thrown out of work in the US Pacific Northwest due to concern that logging in the National Forests would cause the owl's extinction. Since that time, in just a few short years, it has been shown by actual field observations that there are more than twice as many spotted owls in the public forests of Washington state than were thought to be theoretically possible when those loggers lost their jobs. More importantly, it is now evident that spotted owls are capable of living and breeding in landscapes that are dominated by second growth forests. Over 1000 spotted owls have been documented on Simpson Timber's half million acre second growth redwood forests in northern California. And yet, in reporting on the settlement of the Headwaters redwood forests nearby, the *New York Times* described the spotted owl as a "nearly extinct species" despite the fact that there are tens of thousands of them thriving in the forests of the Pacific Northwest. . . .

There is a reason why forestry seldom, if ever, causes species to become extinct. We tend to think that forests need our help to recover after destruction, whether by fire or logging. Of course this is not the case. Forests have been recovering by

Patrick Moore (center), chairman and chief scientist for Greenspirit, advocates logging as an environmentally friendly, renewable source of energy. Deborah Coleman/Stringer/Getty Images News/Getty Images

themselves, without any assistance, from fires, volcanoes, landslides, floods and ice ages, ever since forests began over 350 million years ago. . . .

Clearcutting Is Not Deforestation

My grandfather, Albert Moore, clearcut large areas of coastal rainforest on northern Vancouver Island in the 1930's and '40s. He didn't know the word ecology, and the word biodiversity would not be invented for another 50 years. And you can be sure they weren't talking about the environment at the breakfast table on a dark, cold winter morning before they went out and worked hard six or seven days a week, to get the big timber down to the sea, sometimes taking half the soil with it due to the primitive logging methods of the day. Today these areas are covered in lush new forest in which bears, wolves, cougar, deer, owls, eagles, ravens, and hawks have found a home again. These species have dispersed back to the site as the environment became suitable for them again.

We have all been taught since we were children that you should not judge a book by its cover, in other words that beauty is only skin deep. Yet we are still easily tricked into thinking that if we like what we see with our eyes, it must be good, and if we don't like what we see with our eyes, it must be bad. We tend to link our visual impression of what is beautiful and what is ugly with our moral judgment of what is right and wrong. The Sierra Club says, "You don't need a professional forester to tell if a forest is mismanaged—if a forest appears to be mismanaged, it is mismanaged." They want you to believe that the ugly appearance of a recently harvested forest is synonymous with permanent destruction of the environment. And yet, the unsightly sea of stumps is not nuclear waste or a toxic discharge, it is 100 percent organic, and will soon grow back to a beautiful new forest again. All the same, the fact that recently harvested areas of forest appear ugly to our eyes makes for very effective images in the hands of anti-forestry activists. . . .

A rural scene of farmlands and pasture looks pleasant to the eye and is neat and tidy compared to the jumble of woody debris in a clearcut. Yet it is the farm and pasture land that truly represents deforestation. It has been cleared of forest long ago and the forest has been permanently replaced by food crops and fodder. More important, if we stopped plowing the farmland for just 5 years in a row, seeds from the surrounding trees would blow in and the whole area would be blanketed in new tree seedlings. Within 80 years you would never know there had been a farm there. The entire area would be reforested again, just by leaving it alone. That's because deforestation is not an event, that just happens and then is over forever. Deforestation is actually an ongoing process of continuous human interference, preventing the forest from growing back, which it would if it was simply left alone. The most common form of interference with forest renewal is what we call agriculture. That's why deforestation is seldom caused by forestry, the whole intention of which is to cause reforestation. Deforestation is nearly always caused by friendly farmers growing our food, and by nice carpenters building our houses, towns, and cities. Deforestation is not an evil plot, it is something we do on purpose in order to feed and house the 6 billion and growing human population.

The scene of cattle grazing in a lush green pasture is pleasant to the eye. Yet it wasn't that many years ago when McDonald's restaurants, bowing to heavy public pressure due to concern about deforestation in Central and South America to grow cows for hamburger, promised they would never buy another tropical cow. It was apparently fine, however, to continue buying cows grown in North America. Is this because we have a higher standard for deforestation in North America than they do in Latin America? No, it is a complete double standard. Deforestation is deforestation regardless of where it is practiced. The forest is completely removed and replaced with a monoculture pasture on which exotic animals that were not present in the original forest graze.

If you go to Australia, you'll find that most people think the worst deforestation is occurring in Malaysia and Indonesia, when in fact about 40 percent of Australia's native forest has been destroyed for agriculture. The same is true in the United States; about 40 precent of the original forests have been converted to farming. We always like to think that the bad people are long way away and speak another language. We often fail to realize that we are doing exactly the same things we accuse them of doing.

And if you don't eat meat, you must eat vegetables in which case you will cause the creation of monoculture cabbage plantations and other such food crops where there once were forests. Now it's true that cabbages are prettier than stumps, unfortunately true for the public's understanding of deforestation. Birds and insects are not welcome in areas of monoculture crops. If they wish to avoid being shot or poisoned they had best retreat into a forest nearby where they are more likely to be left alone.

Solutions for Deforestation

Don't get me wrong, I'm not against farming. We all have to eat. But it is interesting to note that the three things we can do to prevent further loss of the world's forests have nothing to do with forestry. These three things are:

1. Population management. The more people there are in this world the more mouths there are to feed and the more forest we must clear to feed them. This is a simple fact of arithmetic.

2. Intensive agricultural production. Over the last 50 years in North America we have learned to grow five times as much food on the same area of land, due to advances in genetics, technology, and pest control. If we had not made these advances we would either have to clear away five times as much forest, which is not available anyway, or more likely we simply could not grow as much food. Again, it is a matter of arithmetic. The more food we can grow on a given piece of land, the less forest will be lost to grow it.

3. Urban densification. There is actually only one significant cause of continuing forest loss in the United States; 200 cities sprawling out over the landscape and permanently converting forest and farm to pavement. If we would design our cities for a higher density, more livable environment, we would not only save forests, we would also use less energy and materials. . . .

Forestry Is Good for the Environment

You would think that since forestry is the most sustainable of all the primary industries, and that wood is without a doubt the most renewable material used to build and maintain our civilization, that this would give wood a lot of green eco-points in the environmental movement's ledger. Unfortunately, this doesn't seem to be the case. Greenpeace has gone before the United Nations Inter-Governmental Panel on Forests, calling on countries to reduce the amount of wood they use and to adopt "environmentally appropriate substitutes" instead. No list of substitutes is provided. The Sierra Club is calling for "zero cut" and an end to all commercial forestry on federal public lands in the United States. The Rainforest Action Network wants a 75 percent reduction in wood use in North America by the year 2015. I think it is fair to summarize this approach as "cut fewer trees, use less wood". It is my firm belief, as a lifelong environmentalist and ecologist, that this is an anti-environmental policy. Putting aside, for a moment, the importance of forestry for our economy and communities; on purely environmental grounds the policy of "use less wood" is anti-environmental. In particular, it is logically inconsistent with, and diametrically opposed to, policies that would bring about positive results for both climate change and biodiversity conservation. I will explain my reasoning for this belief:

> First, it is important to recognize that we do use a tremendous amount of wood. On a daily basis, on average, each of the 6 billion people on Earth uses 3.5 pounds or 1.6 kilos of wood every day, for a total of 3.5 billion tons per year. So why don't we just cut that in half and save vast areas of forest from harvesting? In order to demonstrate the superficial nature of this apparent logic it is necessary to look at what we are doing with all this wood.

It comes as a surprise to many people that over half the wood used every year is not for building things but for burning as energy. 60 percent of all wood use is for energy, mainly for cooking and heating in the tropical developing countries where 2.5 billion people depend on wood as their primary source of energy. They cannot afford substitutes because most of them make less than $1000 per year. But even if they could afford substitute fuels they would nearly always have to turn to coal, oil, or natural gas; in other words non-renewable fossil fuels. How are we going to stabilize carbon dioxide emissions from excessive use of fossil fuels under the Climate Change Convention if 2.5 billion people switch from a renewable wood energy to non-renewable fossil fuels? Even in cases where fuel-wood supplies are not sustainable at present levels of consumption the answer is not to use less wood and switch to non-renewables. The answer is to grow more trees.

Using Less Wood Is Anti-Environmental

25 percent of the wood used in the world is for building things such as houses and furniture. Every available substitute is non-renewable and requires a great deal more energy consumption to produce. That is because wood is produced in a factory called the forest by renewable solar energy. Wood is essentially the material embodiment of solar energy. Non-renewable building materials such as steel, cement, and plastic must be produced in real factories such as steel mills, cement works, and oil refineries. This usually requires large inputs of fossil fuels inevitably resulting in high carbon dioxide emissions. So, for 70 percent of the wood used each year for energy and building, switching to substitutes nearly always results in increased carbon dioxide emissions, contrary to climate change policy.

15 percent of the wood harvested is used to manufacture pulp and paper mainly for printing, packaging, and sanitary purposes. Fully half of this wood is derived from the wastes from the sawmills which produce the solid wood products for building. Most of the remaining supply is from tree plantation's many of which are established on land that was previously cleared for agriculture. So even if we did stop using wood to make pulp and paper it would not have the effect of "saving" many forests. Many of you have heard of the idea that we should stop using trees to make paper and use "alternative fi-

bers" such as hemp, kenaf, and cotton. "Tree-free paper" made from "wood-free pulp" would supposedly be better for the environment than paper made from trees. I speak at schools and universities on a regular basis and have found that many young people believe that this is the right approach to improve the environment. I ask them "where are you going to grow the hemp, on Mars? Do you have another continent somewhere that we don't know about?" No, the fact is we would have to grow the hemp on this planet, in soil where you could otherwise be growing trees.

Give me an acre of land anywhere on Earth, tell me to grow something there with which I can make paper, that would also be best for biodiversity, and I will plant trees every single time, without exception. It is simply a fact that even the simplest monoculture pine plantation is better for wildlife, birds, and insects than any annual farm crop. It is ridiculous for environmental groups who say their main concern is biodiversity conservation to be advocating the establishment of massive monocultures of annual exotic farm crops where we could be growing trees.

It is therefore clear to me that the policy of "use less wood" is anti-environmental because it would result in increased carbon dioxide emissions and a reduction in forested land. I believe the correct policy is a positive rather a negative one. From an environmental perspective the correct policy is "grow more trees, and use more wood". . . .

A World Without Forests Is Unthinkable

To conclude, let me take you back to the rainforest of the West Coast of North America. About 300 feet from my house in downtown Vancouver is Pacific Spirit Park, 2000 acres of beautiful native forest, right in the heart of the city. It is not a botanical garden where people come and prune the bushes and plant tulip bulbs, it is the real thing, a wild west coast rainforest full of Douglas-fir, western red cedar, hemlock, maple, alder, and cherry. But people who come by the hundreds each day to walk on the many trails in Pacific Spirit Park would find it hard to believe that all 2000 acres were completely clearcut logged around the turn of the century to feed the sawmills that helped build Vancouver.

The loggers who clearcut Pacific Spirit Park with double-bitted axes and crosscut saws long before the chainsaw was invented didn't know the words ecology or biodiversity any more than my grandfather did on the north end of Vancouver Island. They just cut the timber and moved on to cut more somewhere else. Nothing was done to help restore the land, but it was left alone. It became part of the University of British Columbia Endowment Lands, and was not developed into housing like the rest of Vancouver. It all grew back into a beautiful new forest and in 1989 was declared a regional park.

In Pacific Spirit Park, there are Douglas-firs over four feet in diameter and over 120 feet tall. All of the beauty has returned to Pacific Spirit Park. The fertility has returned to the soil. And the biodiversity has recovered; the mosses, ferns, fungi, liverworts, and all the other small things that are part of a natural forest. There are pileated woodpeckers, barred owls, ravens, hawks, eagles, coyotes, and a colony of great blue herons nesting in the second-growth cedar trees. It is a forest reborn, reborn from what is routinely described in the media as the "total and irreversible destruction of the environment". I don't buy that. I believe that if forests can recover by themselves from total and complete destruction, that with our growing knowledge of forest science in silviculture, biodiversity conservation, soils, and genetics; we can ensure that the forests of this world continue to provide an abundant, and hopefully growing, supply of renewable wood to help build and maintain our civilization while at the same time providing an abundant, and hopefully growing, supply of habitat for the thousands of other species that depend on the forest for their survival every day just as much as we do. The fact is, a world without forests is as unthinkable as a day without wood.

And it's time that politicians, environmentalists, foresters, teachers, journalists, and the general public got that balance right. Because we must get it right if we are going to achieve sustainability in the 21st century.

Why the Arctic Refuge Should Be Preserved

Jim DiPeso

In this piece Jim DiPeso, policy director of Republicans for Environmental Protection (REP), describes his trip to Alaska's National Wildlife Arctic Refuge in 2004 and shows how the visit helped solidify his group's objections to opening the area to oil drilling. DiPeso depicts the beautiful, pristine lands of the Arctic Refuge, filled with bear, caribou, and golden eagles. He contrasts this picture with Prudhoe Bay, a hub of oil production that is littered with pipelines, airstrips, noise, barrels, trucks, cars, and dust. He argues that opening up the refuge for oil drilling as proposed by President George W. Bush would only make a small dent in America's oil crisis and not provide any lasting solutions. Oil drilling would lead to the loss of one of America's most beautiful wild places, he writes. Congress approved Bush's energy bill in 2005 but stripped it of the provision that would have opened the Arctic for oil drilling. Founded in 1995, Republicans for Environmental Protection works to protect America's natural heritage and environment through support of conservation policies and programs. DiPeso worked as a newspaper reporter and editor before going to work in the nonprofit sector.

There is nothing like an Alaska experience to make an individual feel small. And that's a good thing.

In the Great Land, nature's colossal scale dissolves all human pretensions. The monumental size and wildness of the Alaskan landscape takes hold of your awareness in ways that even the most impressive of man's works cannot.

Big mountains. Alaska's ranges are bracing redoubts of rock, cold, and remoteness, boasting peaks higher than better-known massifs in the Lower 48.

Big wetlands. The Copper River Delta joins land and sea in a 700,000-acre paradise for millions of shorebirds and fleets of fat salmon.

Big forests. The Tongass National Forest is part of the largest coastal temperate rainforest on Earth.

Big ice. Alaska glaciers could swallow entire human settlements.

And a big wildlife refuge. At 19 million acres, the Arctic National Wildlife Refuge is the largest protected place in a conservation system established 101 years ago by Theodore Roosevelt. The refuge contains six distinct ecological zones and is home to bears, caribou, musk oxen, Dall sheep, wolves, foxes, and dozens of less celebrated creatures. The refuge hosts nearly 200 species of migratory birds from all over the world.

A national argument has raged on whether the refuge should be opened to oil drilling. The debate goes deeper than policy issues such as energy security or wildlife conservation. It speaks to deep-seated, sometimes conflicting ethos about the land—the freedom to tap its riches for today, the responsibility to conserve its vitality for future generations.

REP America stands strongly for protection. In a world grown more crowded, stressful, and artificial, the refuge is one of the few places in America where the primal forces that gave rise to life and beauty can be experienced on an epic scale. We are convinced that lasting solutions to our nation's energy problems can be found without turning our last wild places into regretful memories of a lost heritage.

There is nothing like personal experience to strengthen the force of such arguments. So, we—REP America President Martha Marks, Ohio REP Coordinator Fran Buchholzer and I, REP's Policy Director—gladly accepted an invitation offered by the Juneau-based Alaska Coalition to see the refuge for ourselves.

An Introduction to Wild Beauty

A trip to the Alaska wilderness requires preparation for any eventuality, even in the summer. My outfit included waterproof boots, hiking boots, rain gear, thermal underwear, jacket, gloves, wool cap, wool socks, and wool sweater. With body prepared, I brought a volume of essays about the Arctic refuge to prepare my mind.

A Fairbanks motel lobby was the staging area where our group of eight Arctic explorers packed our gear for the trip. We headed to the bush plane terminal in a van loaded with tents, food, and two deflated river rafts ... our possessions and equipment packed into dry bags—waterproof containers rolled tight and latched down.

Traveling on bush planes is not for the impatient. Pilots are ready when they're ready; planes leave when they leave. No sense fretting. Relax and get acquainted with your trip mates.

Which, in addition to Martha, Fran and me, included:

- Dan Ritzman, our lead trip guide and campaign director for the Alaska Coalition in Washington, DC;

- John McWhorter, a guide affiliated with Arctic Wild, our trip outfitter;

- Chris Soderstrom, the Alaska Coalition's public affairs director;

- Brad Stone, a *Newsweek* reporter checking out the refuge for a spread about energy issues that the magazine plans to publish;

- David Klein, a voluble Arctic biologist, new retired from the University of Alaska-Fairbanks.

On the first bush plane, we flew north, crossed the Arctic Circle, and landed in Arctic Village, a Gwich'in settlement at the southern edge of the Arctic National Wildlife Refuge. The Gwich'in are natives whose lives and culture have been woven around the refuge's caribou for thousands of years.

A cheerful local named Joel gave us a quick tour of the village, including a 1920s-era church being renovated.

The next bush plane was piloted by Dirk Nikisch, a colorful sort with a talent for plain speaking, little use for bloviating politicians, and a skilled hand at the controls of his half-century-old, single-engine plane.

Dirk put us down on the tundra. There we were, at 69 degrees north in the Arctic National Wildlife Refuge.

First Impressions—Spongy ground, a treat to walk, sit and lie on.

A vast expanse of sedges, fireweed, low-lying willows, mosses, lichens, wildflowers and grasses stretching across plains and gentle rises to the spectacular Shublik and Sadlerochit Mountains to the south and east. Light breeze, blue sky, cool temperatures, natural quiet. A short distance to the west, the steady gurgling of the Canning River flowing north toward the Arctic Ocean.

Nature at its wildest, wholly primitive. I could have been transported back in time a thousand years and not known the difference.

Second impressions—We were experiencing a wilderness, where, in the eloquent language of the Wilderness Act, "man is a visitor who does not remain." But bears remain. Brown bears, quite large and quite fast on the run. Bear lessons: No food in any tent. If a bear approaches, stand your ground. If the bear moves closer, act bizarrely, shouting and waving your arms. Never run. Have your "bear bomb" pepper spray ready at all times. Spray if the bear closes to within 10 to 15 feet.

We saw no bears on the trip. Too bad for us, lucky for them.

Third impressions—Professor Klein unrolled his maps and gave a lesson on the oil development issue. Oil beneath the refuge's coastal plain is likely to be sitting in small pools. Extracting it would require an infrastructure of drilling pads, pipelines, processing facilities, dormitories, utility lines, roads and airstrips.

Interior Secretary Gale Norton insists that oil development would affect only a small portion of the refuge. Look at the bigger picture, Klein suggested. Oil development would open the door to wider coastal development that would upset the coastal plain's entire ecosystem of plants, rivers, wetlands, and wildlife.

Fourth impressions—Through Klein's spotting scope, we saw bands of caribou scooting across the tundra. Both male and female caribou have antlers, although the males' head gear is larger and more elaborate. They are curious creatures. Every so often, a few stopped to stare at us, then moved on. At a post-dinner walk east of the river, blueberry plants offered a modest Arctic dessert. More caribou were marching toward the river, answering inner imperatives that we could only guess at.

Former Interior Secretary Fred Seaton, who persuaded President Eisenhower to establish the Arctic Wildlife Range in 1960, said the coastal plain is "one of the world's great wildlife areas." He was right.

Current Interior Secretary Norton, who is responsible for the refuge's stewardship on behalf of her 295 million employers, was once quoted as saying that the coastal plain is "not beautiful." She is wrong.

Rafting Through Wild Bird Habitat

Strike the tents, re-pack the dry bags, inflate and load the rafts. We set off on two days of rafting down the Canning River. The river is a gentle float free of demanding rapids, allowing visitors to appreciate the passing views—big sky, circling birds, rolling tundra, mother caribou with calves, and freedom from technological noise.

Gulls shrieked at our presence, prodding us to move along. Golden eagles soared above the riverbank. Long-tailed jaegers showed off their odd plumage as they flew above the river's gentle riffles.

Swooping and circling, Arctic terns displayed their crisp, fork-tailed form. Arctic terns are the class of the migratory bird world. They breed in the Arctic, then head south for the winter . . . way south, all the way to the Antarctic. Every year, Arctic terns fly more than 20,000 miles.

As the rafts floated downstream, the mountain ranges south of the coastal plain receded. Spread before us was a panorama with the look and feel of America's short-grass heartland in olden times—a sweeping vista of immense plains and big sky. During the afternoon lunch break, we took off our boots and savored the soft tundra vegetation between our toes.

The Arctic is not normally associated with barefoot frolics, but the weather was unusually warm. This far north, summer is supposed to be a one-act play. Lately, however, Arctic summers have become longer—melting glaciers, thinning pack ice, thawing permafrost, and drying out forests in Alaska's interior. Natives with generations of experience note that wildlife look unhealthy and are behaving strangely.

To the river's east lay the Arctic refuge's "1002 area"—Section 1002 of the Alaska National Interest Lands Conservation Act. The law forbids oil production and leasing in the 1.5 million-acre 1002 area without an act of Congress. An energy bill approved by the House in 2003 would grant such authorization. A bipartisan majority in the Senate has resisted, to their great credit.

To the river's west lay Alaska state lands not under federal restrictions. We spotted abandoned 55-gallon oil drums and test wells.

Mosquitoes—uncharismatic minor fauna that thrive in the boggy conditions of the coastal plain—appeared at camp the second night. To mosquitoes, your carbon dioxide exhalations are a dinner bell. Up from the tundra they flew at each passing breath.

Despite the winged tormentors, dinner was superb. The trip guides handled food preparation like master chefs. For breakfast, hot oatmeal. Lunches were deli picnics served during rafting breaks: meats, cheeses, crackers, and candies laid out on a blanket. Dinners were camp gourmet—burritos the first night, pasta the second; stir-fry on rice on the third. Between meals, snack attacks were satisfied with gorp, a tasty concoction of nuts and chocolate.

Some of the best dining around can be had on river rafting trips. There's a technical term for it—float and bloat.

As the evening progressed, the sun wheeled toward the north, teasing the horizon, but never quite slipping below at this high latitude. There is no need for a watch to keep your time bearings when the sun is always out. Once you're oriented spatially, the sun can serve as a fine analog clock.

But who's counting? Severed from their technological context, minutes and seconds lose meaning in the wild. You eat when you're hungry and sleep when you're tired. The rhythms of the body re-connect to the rhythms of nature, calming the rhythms of too-busy minds.

Waterfalls and Permafrost

Last day for paddling north. A cold wind kicked up as we neared the Arctic Ocean. Both boats struggled to pass through gravelly shallows. Miniature waterfalls poured from the cut banks, dropping water into the river from the water table lying above the permafrost.

Water is a precious commodity on the tundra. Eight to nine months of snow cover belies the fact that snowfall is relatively scant. Gravel mining for oilfield development would drastically change riparian areas that are critical components of the coastal plain ecosystem.

We had paddled as far north as the guides thought wise. Beyond, as the Canning approaches the Arctic Ocean, the river splits into numerous channels, slowing the current dramatically.

We climbed a bluff, then took a leisurely walk eastward up a long rise into the coastal plain. The enormous vista offered a view of mountains hulking to the south. To the north, a low cloudbank covered the edge of the continent. Beyond lay the ocean and pack ice. Next landfall: Spitzbergen, Europe's northernmost place.

Cirrus clouds drifted across the sky. Bogs, puddles, and meltwater lakes held precious water for the tundra food web. An easterly wind bent delicate cotton flowers, sending their seed elsewhere on the coastal plain to start a new generation. A spectacle of open space and timelessness, what Theodore Roosevelt called the "lonely freedom" to be had in the "wide, waste spaces of the Earth."

At riverside afterwards, a willow ptarmigan cruised along the gravel. At dinner, a plump ground squirrel, dubbed "El Gordo," amused us by begging for scraps. Like all prey, El Gordo lives a staccato, skittish life. Even in their burrows, ground squirrels are not safe. Bears will excavate burrows looking for meat.

Early morning. Dawn, if there is such a thing where the sun never sets. I walked slowly across the tundra and kept an eye out for bears. Here, bears are kings of the roost. Edgy watchfulness for their presence imparts a lesson in grace, humility, and respect that only wilderness can teach. Walk slowly, douse the mental chatter, look around, and soak in the clean sights, slow time, and unforgettable impressions of sky, land, water, and quiet—the original wild America. This is the Arctic National Wildlife Refuge.

Deadhorse Contrast

It was time to leave the refuge to the bears, birds, and caribou. A bush plane took us to our next stop, Prudhoe Bay and the town of Deadhorse, Alaska.

The contrast with the refuge was jarring. Pipelines, roads, airstrips, noise, bustle, barrels, trucks, cars, dust, fumes, fences, rules, regulations, smelly restrooms, bad cafeteria food, and worst of all, television. The only charm came from Denver, a plump tabby that is Deadhorse's one and only pet cat. Denver even has his own souvenir T-shirt, on sale at the general store where he hangs out.

Prudhoe is the nucleus of an oil production complex sending nearly 1 million barrels of oil a day down the Trans-Alaska Pipeline. The "slope," as the workers call it, accounts for nearly 20 percent of U.S. production.

Oil production is a heavy industry requiring powerful equipment, large work crews, and complex infrastructure. One look at Prudhoe tells you there is no way an oil production complex could be tiptoed into the Arctic refuge without disfiguring the place.

Ironies abound. Oil was an unavoidable necessity for enjoying the Arctic refuge. Oil refined into fuel transported us to and from the tundra. Oil was feedstock for polymers fabricated into our camping equipment and the very clothes on our backs.

It is too simplistic to blame America's high oil dependence on politicians or oil companies. Our dangerous ride on an accelerating oil treadmill is the legacy of many decisions, both individual and societal.

Nevertheless, America's current energy diet, with its heavy servings of oil, carries serious risks, like the heart attacks awaiting those who indulge in too many fatty foods.

America is importing more oil as U.S. fields decline and demand soars. Since oil is traded in a global market, price and supply are influenced by faraway events and dysfunctional regimes outside U.S. control. The more we depend on the global oil market, the greater our vulnerability to price shock or supply disruptions.

Rising demand from the U.S., China and other nations is tightening the market, raising price volatility and sowing the seeds of potential conflict. . . .

Leave the Refuge as It Is

Adding a relatively small bucket of Arctic refuge oil to the global petroleum pool would do little to solve this systemic supply-and-demand problem. Drilling the refuge would mean surrendering to old habits rather than finding long-term solutions, like a heart patient who "solves" his weight problem by buying a bigger pair of pants.

Even if the economic issues could be solved, burning oil injects carbon dioxide into the atmosphere. That's risky behavior, because we're tampering with complex atmospheric systems that govern climate.

Climate is the cradle providing hospitable conditions that support human civilization. Rock the cradle and those conditions may change in ways likely to be costly and unpleasant. Early warning bells are ringing in Alaska. Sea levels are rising. Weather patterns are tending toward extremes. Seasonal cues that guide wildlife feeding and reproduction are off kilter.

Old habits depart reluctantly. Patients resist doctors' warnings to change their ways, but delay only makes necessary change that much harder. As writer Bill McKibben likes to say, the laws of physics and the laws of Congress are on a collision course, and the laws of physics are not likely to yield.

Trimming our oil appetite and phasing in a new energy menu will require enough maturity to imagine better alternatives and enough discipline to implement them.

Practicing maturity and discipline means establishing boundaries. Far from being constraining, boundaries break down mental walls, opening the door to fresh thinking.

Leaving the Arctic National Wildlife Refuge just as it is, as nature made it, will establish one such boundary. In the Arctic wilderness, we will find the freedom to make better choices.

Organizations to Contact

American Council on Science and Health (ACSH)
1995 Broadway, 2nd Fl., New York, NY 10023-5860
(212) 362-7044 • fax: (212) 362-4919
e-mail: acsh@acsh.org
Web site: www.acsh.org

ACSH is a consumer education consortium concerned with environmental and health-related issues. The council publishes the quarterly *Priorities*, position papers such as "Global Climate Change and Human Health," and numerous reports, including *Arsenic, Drinking Water, and Health* and *The DDT Ban Turns 30*.

Association for the Study of Literature and the Environment (ASLE)
PO Box 502, Keene, NH 03431
(603) 357-7411
e-mail: asle.us@verizon.net
Web site: www.asle.umn.edu

Founded in 1992 the Association for the Study of Literature and the Environment promotes the exchange of ideas about literature and other cultural representations about the natural world. Its publications include the *ASLE News*, a biannual newsletter reporting ASLE's business and publishing letters from its membership. The newsletter also contains news about conferences, forthcoming publications, and work in progress.

Canadian Centre for Pollution Prevention (C2P2)
100 Charlotte St., Sarnia, ON N7T 4R2
  Canada
(800) 667-9790 • fax: (519) 337-3486
e-mail: info@c2p2online.com
Web site: c2p2online.com

The Canadian Centre for Pollution Prevention is Canada's leading resource on ways to end pollution. It provides access to national and international information on pollution and prevention, online forums, and publications, including *Practical Pollution Training Guide* and the newsletter *at the source*, which C2P2 publishes three times a year.

Cato Institute

1000 Massachusetts Ave. NW
    Washington, DC 20001-5403
(202) 842-0200 • fax: (202) 842-3490
e-mail: cato@cato.org
Web site: www.cato.org

The Cato Institute is a libertarian public policy research foundation that aims to limit the role of government and protect civil liberties. The institute believes EPA regulations are too stringent. Publications offered on the Web site include the bimonthly *Cato Policy Report*, the quarterly journal *Regulation*, the paper "The EPA's Clear Air-ogance," and the book *Climate of Fear: Why We Shouldn't Worry About Global Warming*.

Children's Health Environmental Coalition

12300 Wilshire Blvd., Suite 410
    Los Angeles, CA 90025
(310) 820-2030 • fax: (310) 820-2070
Web site: www.checnet.org

The Children's Health Environmental Coalition (CHEC) is a national nonprofit organization dedicated to educating the public, specifically parents and caregivers, about environmental toxins that affect children's health. CHEC's publications include *First Steps*, a monthly e-mail newsletter that updates parents on environmental toxins in households and communities.

Competitive Enterprise Institute (CEI)

1001 Connecticut Ave. NW, Suite 1250
    Washington, DC 20036

(202) 331-1010 • fax: (202) 331-0640
e-mail: info@cei.org
Web site: www.cei.org

CEI is a nonprofit public policy organization dedicated to the principles of free enterprise and limited government. The institute believes private incentives and property rights, rather than government regulations, are the best way to protect the environment. CEI's publications include the newsletter *Monthly Planet* (formerly *CEI Update*), *On Point* policy briefs, and the books *Global Warming and Other Eco-Myths* and *The True State of the Planet*.

Environmental Justice Resource Center

223 James P. Brawley Dr., Atlanta, GA 30314
(404) 880-6911 • fax: (404) 880-6909
e-mail: ejr@cau.edu
Web site: www.ejrc.cau.edu

Formed in 1994 at Clark Atlanta University, the Environmental Justice Resource Center (EJRC) serves as a research, policy, and information clearinghouse on issues related to environmental justice, race and the environment, civil rights, locations of environmental hazardous industries, land use planning, transportation equity, and suburban sprawl. Center officials assist, support, train, and educate people of color with the goal of facilitating their inclusion into mainstream environmental decision making.

Environmental Protection Agency (EPA)

Ariel Rios Bldg., 1200 Pennsylvania Ave. NW
    Washington, DC 20460
(202) 272-0167
Web site: www.epa.gov

The EPA is the federal agency in charge of protecting the environment and controlling pollution. The agency works toward these goals by enacting and enforcing regulations, identifying and fining polluters, assisting businesses and local environmental agencies, and cleaning up polluted sites. The EPA publishes periodic reports and the monthly *EPA Activities Update.*

Environment Canada

351 St. Joseph Blvd., Gatineau, Quebec K1A 0H3
  Canada
(819) 997-2800 or (800) 668-6767 • fax: (819) 953-2225
e-mail: enviroinfo@ec.gc.ca
Web site: www.ec.gc.ca

Environment Canada is a department of the Canadian government. Its goal is the achievement of sustainable development in Canada through conservation and environmental protection. The department publishes reports, including *Environmental Signals 2003*, and fact sheets on a number of topics, such as acid rain and pollution prevention.

Evangelical Environmental Network (EEN)

10 E. Lancaster Ave., Wynnewood, PA 19096-3495
(202) 554-1955
e-mail: een@creationcare.org
Web site: www.creationcare.org

EEN is an evangelical ministry whose stated purpose is to "declare the Lordship of Christ over all creation" (Col. 1:15-20). Network members encourage the Christian community to work together for true biblical stewardship and protection of the earth's environment. The organization's main publication is *Creation Care*, a magazine established in 1994 and published four times a year.

Foundation for Clean Air Progress (FCAP)

1801 K St. NW, Suite 1000L
  Washington, DC 20036
(800) 272-1604
e-mail: info@cleanairprogress.org
Web site: www.cleanairprogress.org

FCAP is a nonprofit organization that believes the public is unaware of the progress that industry has made in reducing air pollution. The foundation represents various sectors of business and industry in providing information to the public about improving air quality trends. FCAP publishes reports and studies demonstrating that air pollution is on the decline, including *Breathing Easier About Energy—a Healthy Economy and Healthier Air* and *Study on Air Quality Trends, 1970–2015*.

Global Warming International Center (GWIC)
PO Box 50303, Palo Alto, CA 94303
(630) 910-1551 • fax: (630) 910-1561
Web site: www.globalwarming.net

GWIC is an international body that provides information on global warming science and policy to industries and governmental and nongovernmental organizations. The center sponsors research supporting the understanding of global warming and ways to reduce the problem. It publishes the quarterly newsletter *World Resource Review*.

National Resources Defense Council (NRDC)
40 W. Twentieth St., New York, NY 10011
(212) 727-2700 • fax: (212) 727-1773
e-mail: nrdcinfo@nrdc.org
Web site: www.nrdc.org

The NRDC is a nonprofit organization with more than 400,000 members. It uses laws and science to protect the environment, including wildlife and wild places. NRDC publishes the quarterly magazine *OnEarth* (formerly *Amicus Journal*) and hundreds of reports, including *Development and Dollars* and the annual report *Testing the Waters*.

Pew Center on Global Climate Change
2101 Wilson Blvd., Suite 550, Arlington, VA 22201
(703) 516-4146 • fax: (703) 841-1422
Web site: www.pewclimate.org

The Pew Center is a nonpartisan organization dedicated to educating the public and policy makers about the causes and potential consequences of global climate change and informing them of ways to reduce the emissions of greenhouse gases. Its reports include *Designing a Climate-Friendly Energy Policy* and *The Science of Climate Change.*

Property and Environment Research Center (PERC)
2048 Analysis Dr., Suite A, Bozeman, MT 59718
(406) 587-9591
e-mail: perc@perc.org
Web site: www.perc.org

PERC is a nonprofit research and educational organization that seeks market-oriented solutions to environmental problems. The center holds a variety of conferences and provides environmental educational material. It publishes the quarterly newsletter *PERC Reports*, commentaries, research studies, and policy papers, among them *Economic Growth and the State of Humanity* and *The National Forests: For Whom and for What?*

Sierra Club
85 Second St., 2nd Fl.
  San Francisco, CA 94105-3441
(415) 977-5500 • fax: (415) 977-5799
e-mail: information@sierraclub.org
Web site: www.sierraclub.org

The Sierra Club is a grassroots organization with chapters in every state that promotes the protection and conservation of natural resources. The organization maintains separate committees on air quality, global environment, and solid waste, among other environmental concerns, to help achieve its goals. It publishes books, fact sheets, the bimonthly magazine *Sierra* and the *Planet* newsletter, which appears several times a year.

Union of Concerned Scientists (UCS)
2 Brattle Sq., Cambridge, MA 02238
(617) 547-5552 • fax: (617) 864-9405

e-mail: ucs@ucsusa.org
Web site: www.ucsusa.org

UCS aims to advance responsible public policy in areas where science and technology play important roles. Its programs emphasize transportation reform, arms control, safe and renewable energy technologies, and sustainable agriculture. UCS publications include the twice-yearly magazine *Catalyst*, the quarterly newsletter *earthwise*, and the reports *Greener SUVs* and *Greenhouse Crisis: The American Response*.

Worldwatch Institute
1776 Massachusetts Ave. NW
    Washington, DC 20036-1904
(202) 452-1999 • fax: (202) 296-7365
e-mail: worldwatch@worldwatch.org
Web site: www.worldwatch.org

Worldwatch is a nonprofit public policy research organization dedicated to informing the public and policy makers about emerging global problems and trends and the complex links between the environment and the world economy. Its publications include *Vital Signs*, issued every year; the bimonthly magazine *World Watch*; the Environmental Alert series; and numerous policy papers, including *Unnatural Disasters* and *City Limits: Putting the Brakes on Sprawl*.

For Further Research

Books

Joni Adamson, Mei Mei Evans, and Rachel Stein, eds., *The Environmental Justice Reader: Politics, Poetics & Pedagogy*. Tucson: University of Arizona Press, 2002.

Andrew J. Beattie and Paul R. Ehrlich, *Wild Solutions: How Biodiversity Is Money in the Bank*. New Haven, CT: Yale University Press, 2001.

F. Kaid Benfield, Donald D.T. Chen, and Matthew D. Raimi, *Once There Were Greenfields: How Urban Sprawl Is Undermining America's Environment, Economy, and Social Fabric*. New York: Natural Resources Defense Council, 1999.

Eldredge Bermingham, Craig Moritz, and Christopher W. Dick, *Tropical Rainforests: Past, Present, and Future*. Chicago: University of Chicago Press, 2005.

Kathan Brown, *The North Pole*. San Francisco: Crown Point, 2004.

Phil Condon, *Montana Surround: Land, Water, Nature, and Place*. Boulder, CO: Johnson, 2004.

Robert Higgs and Carl P. Close, *Re-Thinking Green: Alternatives to Environmental Bureaucracy*. Oakland: Independent Institute, 2005.

Julie Butterfly Hill, *The Legacy of Luna: The Story of a Tree, a Woman, and the Struggle to Save the Redwoods*. San Francisco: Harper, 2001.

Freeman House, *Totem Salmon: Life Lessons from Another Species*. Boston: Beacon, 1999.

Robert Kirkman, *Skeptical Environmentalism: The Limits of Philosophy and Science.* Bloomington: Indiana University Press, 2002.

James P. Lester, *Environmental Injustice in the United States.* Boulder, CO: Westview, 2001.

Paul Lindholdt and Derrick Knowles, eds., *Holding Common Ground: The Individual and Place in the American West.* Spokane: Eastern Washington University Press, 2005.

Thomas E. Lovejoy and Lee Jay Hannah, *Climate Change and Biodiversity.* New Haven, CT: Yale University Press, 2004.

Gaylord Nelson, Paul R. Wozniak, and Susan Campbell, *Beyond Earth Day: Fulfilling the Promise.* Madison: University of Wisconsin Press, 2002.

Carl Pope and Paul Rauber, *Strategic Ignorance: Why the Bush Administration Is Recklessly Destroying a Century of Environmental Progress.* San Francisco: Sierra Club, 2004.

Adam Rome, *The Bulldozer in the Countryside: Suburban Sprawl and the Rise of American Environmentalism.* Cambridge, MA: Cambridge University Press, 2001.

Periodicals

Jason Best, "Father Nature," *OnEarth*, Summer 2005.

Philip Booth, "Distances/Shallows/Deeps. (Field Notes from an East-Facing Window at the Cold End of a Long Maine Winter)," *Ohio Review*, Spring 2001.

Peter Byrne, "Property and Environment: Thoughts on an Evolving Relationship," *Harvard Journal of Law & Public Policy*, Spring 2005.

Mark L. Clifford, "Rainforest Rescue; Can Sustainable Logging Succeed? A Group Experiment in Indonesia Could Show Big Timber the Way," *Business Week*, October 27, 2003.

Katherine Ellison, "Stopping Traffic. (What Would Jesus Drive?)," *Christian Century*, November 20, 2002.

Gary Gardner, "The Environment as Sacred Ground," *USA Today*, May 2003.

Mark Hertsgaard, "Beyond Boycotts: Targeting Corporations to Prevent Environmental Damage," *Nation*, March 7, 2005.

Elizabeth Kolbert, "The Climate of Man—I," *New Yorker*, April 25, 2005.

Brian Lavendel, "Living Together with Biodiversity: In the Past, Farmers and Ranchers Were Sometimes Seen as a Threat to Biodiversity. Today, They Are Being Asked to Help," *Journal of Soil and Water Conservation*, May/June 2003.

Linda L. Layne, "In Search of Community: Tales of Pregnancy Loss in Three Toxically Assaulted Communities in the U.S.," *Women's Studies Quarterly on Women and Environment*, Spring/Summer 2001.

Jacques Leslie, "Using Narrative to Tell Stories About Water: 'The Imperatives of Narrative Nonfiction Carried Me Like a Current to the Book's Last Words,'" *Nieman Reports*, Spring 2005.

Paul Lindholdt, "Ecological Criticism Today," *Sewanee Review*, Winter 2002.

Luisa Maffi, "Diversity and the Spice of Life. (Biocultural Diversity)," *ReVision*, Fall 2002.

Nicholas O'Connell, "At One with the Natural World—Barry Lopez's Adventure with the Word and the Wild," *Commonweal*, March 24, 2000.

Daniel Patterson, "'I Commend You to Allegany Underbrush': The Subversive Place-Made Self in Elizabeth C. Wright's Treatise on Nature, *Lichen Tufts*," *Legacy: A Journal of American Women Writers*, Winter 2000.

Valerie Richardson, "In Idaho, the Loggers Are Losing: Idahoans Have Watched Their Lumber Industry Grind to a Halt as Environmentalists Use the Courts to Stop Logging in National Forests. Meanwhile, Locals Struggle to Earn a Living," *Insight on the News*, December 24, 2001.

John F. Schumaker, "Earth Warrior: Paul Watson, Co-Founder of Greenpeace," *New Internationalist*, September 2003.

Michael Shellenberger and Ted Nordhaus, "The Death of Environmentalism: Global Warming Politics in a Post-Environmental World," *Grist Magazine On-line*, January 15, 2005. www.grist.org/news/maindish/2005/01/13/doe reprint.

Vandana Shiva, "Special Report: Golden Rice and Neem: Biopatents and the Appropriation of Women's Environmental Knowledge," *Women's Studies Quarterly on Women and Environment*, Spring/Summer 2001.

Elizabeth S. Tapia, "Earth Spirituality and the People's Struggle for Life: Reflection from the Perspectives of Indigenous Peoples," *Ecumenical Review*, July 2002.

Vanessa Timmer and Calestous Juma, "Taking Root: Biodiversity Conservation and Poverty Reduction Come Together in the Tropics: Lessons Learned from the Equator Initiative," *Environment*, May 2005.

Jay Watson, "Economics of a Cracker Landscape: Poverty as an Environmental Issue in Two Southern Writers," *Mississippi Quarterly*, Fall 2002.

W. William Weeks, "Reflections on a Fallen Oak," *Nature Conservancy*, September/October 2000.

Index